KV-458-183

She was sitting on a bench outside the church.

Archie Carew paused as he drew level with her. Even though it was none of his business what she was doing there, he couldn't just walk away.

'Are you all right?' he asked, and saw the start she gave. It was obvious that she hadn't noticed him.

She gave a broken little laugh. 'I'm supposed to be getting married tomorrow. Everything is all arranged—my dress, the cake, the service at this church…'

'But now you're having second thoughts?' he suggested.

She took a deep breath. 'Yes. I just wish I'd listened to what my heart has been telling me before now.'

Archie didn't say anything to that. If *he'd* listened to his heart then he wouldn't be thinking about giving up the career he loved.

She gave him a quick smile, and Archie realised with a sudden jolt just how beautiful she was. With her soft brown hair and huge hazel eyes, she was truly gorgeous.

'If there's any advice I can give you, then it's to follow your heart. If it doesn't feel right in here—' he placed his hand on his chest '—don't do it.'

Archie felt his heart ache as he glanced at her. She looked so vulnerable that he was tempted to stay.

'Good luck,' he said huskily. 'I hope everything works out for you.' He took a deep breath. Even though *he* might not be able to follow his heart, at least he could make amends for what he had done.

The thought made him feel better than he'd done for a long time, and he realised that it was all thanks to this beautiful runaway bride…

Dear Reader

In November 2006 my husband and I experienced the joy of seeing our daughter, Vicky, marry her fiancé, Jamie. The wedding was held in Thailand, and it was the most wonderful day we could have wished for. I decided to mark the occasion by writing this mini-series—four books which all revolve around a wedding.

When Heather Thompson realises the day before her wedding that she is making a mistake, she doesn't know what to do. How can she call off the wedding at this stage and let everyone down? However, a chance meeting with a kindly stranger convinces her that it will be even worse if she goes ahead and marries for the wrong reasons.

Cancelling her wedding means that Heather needs to make a lot more changes to her life. She leaves Dalverston and takes a job in London, and is stunned when she finds herself working with the man who helped her make up her mind. It isn't long before she realises that she and Archie Carew are attracted to each other, but is it wise to start another relationship so soon?

Bringing Archie and Heather together during this book was a real pleasure. They were two characters I really loved and enjoyed writing about. I hope you enjoy reading their story, and all the other stories in this series.

Best wishes

Jennifer

For more details visit my website:
www.jennifer-taylor.com

MARRYING THE RUNAWAY BRIDE

BY
JENNIFER TAYLOR

MILLS & BOON®
Pure reading pleasure™

INVERCLYDE LIBRARIES

All the characters in this book have no existence outside
the imagination of the author, and have no relation
whatsoever to anyone bearing the same name or names.
They are not even distantly inspired by any individual
known or unknown to the author, and all the incidents
are pure invention.

All Rights Reserved including the right of reproduction
in whole or in part in any form. This edition is published
by arrangement with Harlequin Enterprises II BV/S.à.r.l.
The text of this publication or any part thereof may
not be reproduced or transmitted in any form or by
any means, electronic or mechanical, including
photocopying, recording, storage in an information
retrieval system, or otherwise, without the written
permission of the publisher.

® and TM are trademarks owned and used by the
trademark owner and/or its licensee. Trademarks marked
with ® are registered with the United Kingdom Patent
Office and/or the Office for Harmonisation in the
Internal Market and in other countries.

First published in Great Britain 2008
Large Print edition 2008
Harlequin Mills & Boon Limited,
Eton House, 18-24 Paradise Road,
Richmond, Surrey TW9 1SR

© Jennifer Taylor 2008

ISBN: 978 0 263 19995 6

Set in Times Roman 16¾ on 21 pt.
17-1208-46099

Printed and bound in Great Britain
by Antony Rowe Ltd, Chippenham, Wiltshire

Jennifer Taylor lives in the north west of England, in a small village surrounded by some really beautiful countryside. She has written for several different M&B series in the past, but it wasn't until she read her first Medical™ Romance that she truly found her niche. She was so captivated by these heart-warming stories that she set out to write them herself!

When not writing, or doing research for her latest book, Jennifer's hobbies include reading, gardening, travel, and chatting to friends, both on and off-line. She is always delighted to hear from readers, so do visit her website at www.jennifer-taylor.com

Recent titles by the same author:

THE SURGEON'S FATHERHOOD SURPRISE**
THEIR LITTLE CHRISTMAS MIRACLE
DR FERRERO'S BABY SECRET*
DR CONSTANTINE'S BRIDE*

**Brides of Penhally Bay*
Mediterranean Doctors

For The Wedding Party: Vicky and Jamie,
Kathy, Carl, Pauline, John, Nigel, Neil,
Mark, Mel. And last but never least, Bill.
Thank you all for an unforgettable day.

CHAPTER ONE

Dalverston: December

SHE was sitting on a bench outside the church. The wind was bitter as it blew down from the surrounding hills, but she seemed oblivious to the icy conditions as she sat there, lost in thought. Archie Carew paused as he drew level with her. Even though he knew it was none of his business what she was doing there, he couldn't just walk away.

It had been pure impulse that had made him decide to spend the night in Dalverston, a bustling little market town on the borders of Lancashire and Cumbria. It was a long drive back to London from his family home in Scotland at the best of times, but at this time of the year, when everyone was out doing their Christmas shopping, the journey had been horrendous. The thought of being cooped up in the car any longer had been more than he could bear so he had left the motorway and booked himself into a hotel. Once he had taken his case up to his room, he had decided to go for a walk and that's when he had seen her.

Archie sighed as he studied the expression on her face. He knew how it felt to sink to that level of despair. The past eighteen months had been a nightmare, several times he'd wondered if he would get through them. He had buried himself in his job in the hope that it would blot out the pain, but it had been inevitable that he would have had to deal with it at some point.

That's what he'd been doing for the past three weeks, sorting out the mess that had been left behind after his brother's death. The situation was far worse than he'd imagined, too. It would need drastic measures to put things right. Archie knew that his whole life would have to change and it was hard to accept that fact. However, for the moment he was more concerned about the young woman than about himself.

'Are you all right?' he asked and saw the start she gave. It was obvious that she hadn't noticed him and it merely reinforced his suspicions that something terrible had happened. Although he wasn't sure if he should get involved, he sat down beside her.

'Is there anything I can do? Sometimes it helps if you talk about a problem.'

She gave a broken little laugh. 'I don't think talking will help in this instance.'

'Maybe not, but why not give it a shot?' He shrugged when she looked at him. 'You've nothing to lose, and I promise you that I'm a very good listener.'

'You're very kind, but I wouldn't know where to start.'

'The beginning is usually the best place,' he said lightly, and she sighed.

'That's the whole point, though. Everything was fine in the beginning. I was so sure I was doing the right thing, and then last week, I started to wonder if I was making a mistake…'

She trailed off but Archie didn't press her. He could tell that she was on the verge of tears so waited until she felt able to continue. After a few seconds had elapsed she carried on.

'I'm supposed to be getting married tomorrow. Everything is all arranged. It has been for months—my dress, the cake, the service here at this church and the reception afterwards. There's over a hundred guests coming and several of them are travelling some distance to get here, too.'

'But now you're having second thoughts?' he suggested when once again she faltered.

'Yes. I know it's crazy. I mean, how on earth can I call off the wedding at this stage?'

'I understand how difficult it must be,' Archie said quietly. 'But surely the question you should be asking yourself is how can you go ahead with it if you have any doubts.'

'I know. And it's something I've asked myself a dozen times, too, but it hasn't helped. I just don't know what to do for the best!'

Archie sighed when he saw her shoulders heave as she started to cry. Reaching over, he squeezed her hand. 'A lot of people have last-minute jitters before they get married. That's probably all this is, too. Why don't you go and see your fiancé and talk it all through with him? I'm sure it would help.'

'No.' She ran a trembling hand over her face to wipe away her tears. 'I need to decide for myself what I want to do. If I speak to Ross, I'll only end up feeling guilty about letting him down.'

'You aren't letting anyone down,' Archie said

firmly. 'You certainly can't go ahead with the wedding just so you won't upset him. You'd be letting yourself down then and that wouldn't be right, would it?'

'No, it wouldn't.' She took a deep breath. 'Thank you. I needed someone to tell me that even though I already knew it deep down inside. I just wish I'd had the courage to listen to what my heart has been telling me before now.'

Archie didn't say anything to that. If *he* listened to his heart then he wouldn't be thinking about giving up the career he loved. All his life he had wanted only one thing and that had been to help sick children get better. Whereas most of his friends at med school had chosen their specialities towards the end of their studies, he had known from the outset what he'd wanted to do.

He had worked incredibly hard since he had qualified, too, but his efforts had paid off last year when he'd been appointed head of paediatric care at one of London's top teaching hospitals. It was the job he had dreamed about and it was bitterly ironic that he was going to have to give it up now.

It was too painful to deal with that thought right then. He turned to the young woman again, wondering why it seemed so important that he should help her. Whatever decision she made would have little impact on his life, yet he desperately wanted her to make the right choice.

'So what do you intend to do? If you don't want to speak to your fiancé, is there anyone else you can talk to? A friend, perhaps, or your parents? What about your mother? Surely she could advise you?'

'My mother's dead. There's just my dad now and he was thrilled about me and Ross getting married.' She bit her lip and he could tell that tears were threatening again. 'He'll be so upset if I call off the wedding.'

'You can't let that influence you,' Archie said

decisively. 'All right, so maybe it would have been better if you'd realised you were making a mistake before now, but it will be a whole lot worse if you go through with this wedding and regret it later.'

'You're right, of course you are. It will be much, much worse for everyone.'

She gave him a quick smile and Archie realised with a sudden jolt just how beautiful she was. With her soft brown hair curling around her heart-shaped face and those huge hazel eyes fringed by incredibly thick black lashes, she was truly gorgeous.

Quite frankly, the discovery was enough to stun any man into silence, but it was the fact that he had noticed how she looked that shocked him most of all. Since Stephanie had died in the same tragic accident that had claimed his brother's life, he hadn't looked at another woman, hadn't been interested in looking either. However, all of a sudden he was so aware of the woman sitting beside him that he could feel his body thrumming with sexual tension.

He stood up abruptly, disgusted with himself for the way he was behaving. 'I have to go. I hope you'll think about what we've said, though, and not rush into a decision. You need to consider everything and make sure it's not just last-minute nerves that's causing you to have these doubts.'

'I shall. Thank you. You've been very kind, letting me pour out my troubles like that.'

'I was glad to help.'

'Why?' She gave a little shrug. 'We're complete strangers so why should you want to help me? Most people wouldn't want to get involved, so what makes you any different?'

'Let's just say that I know how it feels to be forced into doing something you don't want to do.'

'Because it's happened to you?' she said softly, and he nodded.

'Yes. And if there's any advice I can give you, it's to follow your heart. If it doesn't feel right in here…' he placed his hand on his heart '…don't do it.'

'That's what I'm going to do.' She stood up and there seemed to be a new resolve in her eyes when she looked at him now. 'I'm going to follow my heart and see where it leads me instead of doing what I think is right all the time.'

'Good.'

Archie couldn't explain why he felt so choked up. Maybe it was relief because she seemed to have reached a decision, or maybe it was more complicated than that, but all of a sudden he was overwhelmed with emotion. He swung round, very much afraid that he would make a fool of himself if he lingered.

'Thank you again…for everything.'

Archie felt his heart ache as he glanced back. She looked so vulnerable as she stood there that he was tempted to stay, but it would be wrong to influence her in any way. She had to decide for herself what she intended to do and all he could do was hope that she wouldn't regret it in the future.

'You're welcome,' he said huskily. 'Good luck. I hope everything works out for you.'

He took a deep breath as he crossed the road, feeling the cold air biting deep into his lungs. For the past eighteen months he had been merely marking time, but now that period was over. Even though *he* might not be able to follow his heart, at least he could make amends for what he had done.

The thought made him feel better than he'd done for a long time, and he realised that it was all thanks to that woman, too. If she could find the courage to reassess her life, he could find the courage to make these changes.

London: March

'We've been really short-staffed since Christmas. At one point we were working double shifts and it was no joke, I can tell you. If our departmental head hadn't put his foot down, we'd have had to keep on doing them, too. He raised a real stink about it and that's why we were given permission to hire agency staff.' The ward sister laughed as she opened the staffroom door. 'It's not a good idea to get on the wrong side of him!'

'Thanks for the warning.'

Heather Thompson smiled as she looked around the room. As hospital staffrooms went, this one wasn't too bad. At least the chairs looked as though the springs weren't all broken and there was actually a rug on the regulation blue composite floor. Compared to some of the hospitals where she'd worked in the last few months, this was quite luxurious, in fact.

'It's not too bad, is it?' The sister must have noticed her taking stock. 'It's not exactly the Ritz, but it's not the absolute pits either. We have our consultant to thank for that too. He insisted on them refurbishing the place when he took over last year, said it wasn't right that staff had to put up with such appalling conditions when they were expected to work twenty-four seven.'

'Really? I am impressed.' Heather hung her coat in an empty locker. 'Most consultants couldn't care less about the staff, in my experience.'

'Oh, he's a real treasure, believe me.' The other woman sighed. 'It's just a shame that he's leaving—'

She broke off when an alarm sounded. Heather recognised the sound immediately and was already on her way to the door before the ward sister could tell her to follow her. Staff were appearing from all over the place, responding to the call. There were half a dozen people gathered by the time they entered the ward, and each and every one seemed to know what was expected of them.

Heather followed the convoy to the child's bed, her heart aching when she saw how young he was. He couldn't have been more than eight years old and he was desperately ill. One of the nurses had already started CPR, another had fetched the crash trolley, while a third was frantically working the controls on the bed to lower it into a horizontal position. It was obvious they had the situation covered so she turned to the boy's parents.

'Let's leave the team to do their job,' she said, urging the couple towards the door.

'But I want to stay!' the mother shrieked. 'Charlie needs me—I can't leave him!'

Heather grasped hold of the woman's arm when she tried to force her way back through the group to get to her son. The last thing the staff needed at the moment was a hysterical parent hampering their efforts to resuscitate the child.

'Charlie needs their help more than anything else,' she said firmly, trying to lead her away.

'Let me go!'

Heather gasped when the woman swung round and struck her across the face. She staggered back, but quickly recovered. Taking a firmer grip on the woman's arm, she ushered her out of the ward, thanking her stars that the boy's father followed them without a murmur. She wouldn't have rated her chances if he'd clobbered her as well!

There was a family room next to the office and she took the parents in there. She managed to persuade them to sit down then got them both a cup of tea from the machine in the corner and sat down opposite them.

'I know how worried you are but the staff are doing everything they can to help Charlie.' She pressed a cup of tea into the woman's hand. 'Try a sip of this. It will help.'

The woman obediently drank a little of the tea. All the fight seemed to have drained out of her now as she sat huddled on the edge of the sofa. 'I thought he was getting better. The doctor said he was, didn't he, Darren?'

'Yes.' The father ran a trembling hand over his face. Heather's heart went out to him when she saw that he was crying.

'I only started working here tonight so I don't know what's wrong with your son,' she explained quietly. 'But I do know that everything possible is being done to help him.'

'One of the nurses said that he'd had a heart attack,' the father told her. He shook his head. 'I know he's been having pains in his chest but I didn't think kids could have heart attacks. I mean, it's something *old* people have, not eight-year-olds like our Charlie.'

'It's unusual, but it does happen,' Heather said gently. 'The main thing is that Charlie was already in hospital when it happened. That will certainly go in his favour.'

'So you think he'll be all right, do you?' the mother said desperately.

'Let's hope so.'

Heather was too experienced to make promises she might not be able to keep. It was impossible to foretell what the outcome would be and all she could do was reassure the parents while they waited for news. It was almost half an hour before the door opened and she stood up when the parents leapt to their feet. Just for a moment she stared at the man who had entered the room, wondering where she had seen him, before all of a sudden it came rushing back and she gasped.

It was the man she had spoken to the day before her wedding! What on earth was he doing here?

CHAPTER TWO

ARCHIE could feel the shock waves reverberating around his body when he saw the woman. He'd thought about her many times since that day they had met. Far too often, in fact, her face had sprung to mind and he had found himself wondering what had happened to her. If he'd known her name, he might have tried to find out, but the lack of information had ruled out that possibility. To suddenly see her right here, in the hospital, stunned him and he had to force himself to focus as he turned to Charlie's parents.

'Why don't we sit down?' he suggested, ushering the couple back into the room. He waited until they had sat down before he turned to the young woman. 'Thank you, Nurse. I'll handle things from here on.'

'Of course, sir.'

She smiled politely as she hurried to the door, but Archie could see the colour in her cheeks and knew that she was as shocked as he was by the unexpected encounter. He could only assume that she was one of the agency nurses, although it seemed strange that fate had brought her here.

'First of all let me assure you that Charlie is fine,' he said, quickly dismissing that thought. He didn't believe in fate. As he knew from experience, a person's life was dictated by the choices he or she made, not by some unforeseen force of nature. 'He suffered a myocardial infarction—a heart attack—but he's stable now and his vital signs are as good as we can hope for at the present time.'

'Thank heavens!'

Charlie's mother started crying when she heard that. Archie passed her the box of tissues off the table and waited while she collected herself. He wanted to be sure both parents understood that their son wasn't in the clear yet.

'We've completed all the tests now and I'm ninety-nine per cent certain that Charlie is suffering from myocarditis, which is a fancy term for inflammation of the heart muscle. You mentioned that he'd had an upper respiratory tract infection before Christmas and I think it can be linked directly to that.'

'You mean that cough he had has caused him to have a heart attack,' the father demanded.

'Basically, that's correct, Mr Maguire,' Archie confirmed. 'The most common cause of myocarditis is a viral infection usually caused by one of the Coxsackie viruses. I think that's what has happened in this instance.'

'But I had loads of coughs and colds when I was a kid,' Darren Maguire protested. 'And I never had a bad heart.'

'No, but sadly Charlie hasn't been as lucky as

you were,' Archie explained patiently, knowing it was a lot for the parents to take in. 'Fortunately, your GP suspected there was a problem when he learned that Charlie had been getting those pains in his chest. It's thanks to him for referring Charlie to us so promptly that we've been able to get to the root of the matter. The tests we've run have shown there is a disturbance in your son's heartbeat and that his heart isn't working as efficiently as it should be doing either. That's why Charlie was complaining of feeling breathless all the time.'

'So what happens now?' Darren Maguire asked. 'Can you give Charlie some drugs to make him better?'

'Unfortunately, there's no specific treatment for myocarditis. Charlie will need bed rest while he recovers and I've also prescribed corticosteroid drugs to reduce the inflammation.' He leant forward, wanting to impress on the parents how serious the situation was. 'The main thing is that Charlie must remain in hospital while we monitor what's happening to him. With rest and the proper care, I'm hopeful that he will make a full recovery, but it will take time. There's no quick fix to this problem, I'm afraid.'

'It doesn't matter how long it takes,' Cheryl Maguire said, wiping her eyes. 'As long as he gets better, that's all that matters, Mr Carew.'

'Indeed it is.' Archie stood up and smiled at them. 'Charlie's having another ECG at the moment. I'll send one of the nurses to fetch you when it's finished.'

'Thank you, Doctor. You've been very kind.' Cheryl bit her lip. 'I feel awful about what happened before. I never meant to hit that poor nurse. I don't know what came over me.'

'You hit one of the staff?' Archie exclaimed.

'Yes. It was the nurse who brought us in here and gave us a cup of tea. She was so kind to us, too…'

Archie sighed as Cheryl trailed off. 'I'm not sure exactly what happened but any display of physical violence towards a member of the hospital's staff will be taken very seriously. I suggest you apologise to the nurse concerned as soon as you get the chance.'

'Oh, I will,' Cheryl said hurriedly.

Archie left the room and went back to the ward. It was almost seven p.m. but there was little chance of him leaving just yet. Fortunately, everything seemed to have calmed down now the crisis was over. Most of the children were watching television or playing with the games' stations he'd had installed for their use. It was open visiting during the day and there were still some parents around. Although he encouraged families to play an active part in their children's recovery, he emphasised that they needed their rest so visiting ended at seven-thirty each evening. Of course, if a child was seriously ill then special arrangements were made.

He checked on Charlie and was pleased with the results of the latest ECG. He asked one of the nurses to fetch the boy's parents in then went to the office. Marion Yates, the ward sister, was writing up the boy's notes; she looked up and smiled at him.

'That was a bit hairy.'

'I didn't think we were going to get him back at one point,' Archie said bluntly, slumping down in a chair. He tipped back his head and groaned. 'It's hard to tell which bit of me is aching the most. Why do emergencies always come along in threes?'

'They're a bit like buses. You wait ages for one to arrive and then they all turn up together,' Marion said, chuckling. She put down her pen and got up to switch on the kettle. 'How about a cuppa? That might help.'

'A long hot bath followed by a full body massage would be better,' Archie grumbled, wiggling his aching shoulders.

'Sorry, no can do. I mean, what would the staff think if they found you stretched out across

the desk with me giving you a massage?'
Marion teased him. 'The gossips would have a
field day!'

'At this precise moment I couldn't care less
what anyone thought,' Archie retorted and then
yawned widely. 'I've been trying to pack after
I finish work and it's no joke, I can tell you. I
don't know where half the stuff has come from.
Every cupboard and drawer seems to be filled
to the brim.'

He yawned again as tiredness caught up with
him. He'd been called into work before six that
morning and it had been non-stop from then on.
It would be after eight before he got home at this
rate and he would have to set to work on sorting
out the rest of his belongings otherwise he
would never get everything done in time for the
move. He closed his eyes as a cloud of gloom
descended on him. Even though he'd set everything in motion, he still couldn't believe that he
was actually going to give up the job he adored,

but he had to get used to the idea. Come the end of March, he would be leaving London and that would be the end of his career as a doctor.

Someone tapped on the office door just then and Archie's eyes flew open. With his head still tipped over the back of the chair, the view of the newcomer was somewhat distorted. From this angle he was seeing her upside down, although he had to admit that starting at the bottom didn't make the picture any less attractive.

A flurry ran through him as he took stock of long legs encased in black cotton trousers, slim hips, a neat waist and a shapely bosom beneath a crisp white uniform jacket. He was really enjoying himself by the time he reached her face and his pleasure didn't dim one iota as he continued his appraisal—a full mouth, a straight little nose, a pair of hazel eyes framed by thick black lashes….

Archie reared up with all the finesse of a rusty spring uncoiling when he realised who she was.

The woman gave him a tight little smile as he stood up and spun round, but he could see the strain on her face and knew she was worried that he was going to say something about how they had met. He took a deep breath and used it to damp down his racing pulse. In that second, he knew that neither thumbscrews nor boiling oil would make him reveal what had happened in Dalverston. Her secret was safe with him. He would never tell a soul.

Heather could feel the tension humming along her nerves and fought to control it. The only way she was going to get through the next few minutes was by staying calm. She fixed a smile to her mouth as she turned to the ward sister.

'Mrs Jackson wants to know if Emily can go home tomorrow. I said that I'd check with you.'

'I'd like to keep her in for at least another day.'

Heather's gaze swivelled sideways when a male voice answered. In a fast sweep her eyes took in the rumpled dark brown hair, the tired green eyes, the firm but beard-shadowed jaw. He was taller than she remembered, his body looking lean and fit beneath the pale grey shirt he was wearing with a pair of darker grey trousers. He looked older and far more careworn than when she had seen him last and the thought bothered her. His kindness that day had been the one bright spot to come out of a very dark experience.

'Sorry. I'd better introduce myself.' He held out his hand, his green eyes looking straight into hers. 'I'm Archie Carew, head of the paediatric unit. I take it that you're one of the agency staff?'

'I…um…that's right,' Heather murmured. She took his hand, feeling the jolt that ran through her as his fingers closed around hers. She wasn't sure what was happening but all of a sudden she felt safer than she'd done for ages. There was something immensely comforting about the firm pressure of his palm against hers. She had the strangest feeling that if she held onto Archie Carew's hand then nothing could ever hurt her.

She took a quick breath as she pulled her hand away. It was ridiculous to get carried away by such a fanciful notion. The only person she could rely on now was herself, not some man she barely knew.

'Heather Thompson,' she said crisply. 'I just started working here tonight.'

'Rather a baptism of fire,' he replied easily. He glanced at the ward sister and raised his brows. 'Apparently, Charlie's mum hit Heather. I don't know if she told you.'

'No, she didn't!' Marion exclaimed. 'You should have said something, Heather.'

'It doesn't matter,' Heather said quickly, because the last thing she wanted was to make a fuss. 'The poor woman was upset and I under-stand that's why it happened.'

'It's good of you to take it that way, but I made it clear to Mrs Maguire that we view these matters extremely seriously,' Archie said firmly. 'I won't have members of staff being assaulted for any reason.'

Heather shrugged. 'I'm sure it won't happen again.' She swiftly changed the subject, loath to get into an argument. 'What should I tell Mrs Jackson? She seems very anxious about taking Emily home.'

'I'll have a word with her,' Archie offered immediately. He turned to Marion and grinned. 'I'll have to take a rain-check on that tea and the massage, I'm afraid.'

He laughed when the sister rolled her eyes. It was obviously an 'in' joke and Heather couldn't help feeling excluded as he followed her out of the office. She sighed. Being out of the loop was something she would have to get used to now that she was doing agency work. Still, the up side was that she wouldn't have to explain herself to anyone and that more than made up for it.

They went back to the ward and Archie

headed straight for Emily's bed. He seemed to have taken it for granted that Heather would go with him so she did. He smiled at Emily's mother when she hurriedly stood up. Heather had noticed how nervous the woman appeared to be when she'd been speaking to her and she was pleased to see that Archie was making allowances for that.

'I believe you were asking if Emily could go home tomorrow, Mrs Jackson,' he said gently.

'That's right. Her…her father is very keen to have her back at home so I said I'd ask you,' the woman whispered, nervously plucking at the cuff of her expensive cashmere sweater.

Heather frowned when she spotted a livid bruise on the woman's wrist. It was obviously a recent injury and it must have been painful, although Mrs Jackson appeared unaware of it.

'I can understand that,' Archie replied soothingly. 'However, I think it would be better if we kept Emily here for another day or so. Her kidney function is almost back to normal but I don't want to take any chances of her relapsing. Another couple of days will make all the difference.'

'If you say so, Doctor,' the woman mumbled.

She quickly gathered up her belongings, said goodbye to Emily and left. Heather smiled at the little girl when she noticed her downcast expression.

'Mummy will be back tomorrow to see you, sweetheart. In the meantime, would you like to watch some television or maybe read a book?'

Emily's big dark eyes fastened hopefully on her face. 'Will you read me a story?' she whispered, sounding exactly like her mother.

'Of course I will!' Heather reached over to hug her, feeling alarm run through her when the child immediately cowered away. It was obvious the little girl had been expecting a blow and there could be only one explanation for it, too.

'I'll go and find you a book then come straight back,' she assured her, glancing at Archie to see if he had noticed Emily's reaction. It was clear from his expression that he had, and that he'd drawn the same conclusion as she had done. He followed her to the dayroom and she could feel the waves of anger emanating from him.

'You noticed it too, didn't you?' she said quietly, crouching down in front of the bookcase.

'The way she cringed when you went to touch her? Yes.' His tone was grim. 'I had my suspicions when Emily was admitted but there was no proof that she'd been injured deliberately. The father's explanation could very easily have been true.'

'What did he say had happened to her?' Heather asked, pulling out a book about Paddington Bear, a particular favourite of hers when she'd been Emily's age.

'He said that Emily had fallen off her scooter in the park and had hurt herself when she'd banged into a tree. The mother backed him up.'

'I read her notes and I know she had severe

bruising to her right kidney when she was admitted.'

'That's right. She was in a bad way when she was brought in—passing blood and in tremendous pain. Although only her right kidney had been damaged, we decided to take the strain off her left one and put her on dialysis while it recovered.' He shook his head. 'It's hard to believe that any parent could do that to their own child.'

'Has she been brought into hospital before?' Heather asked, standing up.

'We don't have any notes for her here, but I'll have a word with the social workers and see if they can check if she's been treated at another hospital. If we can find a history of so-called accidents, it would help to prove that she's being abused.' He sighed. 'They'll need to be quick, though. I can't keep her in here for ever.'

'I noticed that the mother has a really bad bruise on her wrist. It might be worth following that up to see if there's ever been a complaint made about domestic violence by any of their neighbours.'

'Good idea!' he exclaimed and smiled at her. 'I can tell you're going to be an asset to this department. Any chance of you taking a job here on a permanent basis?'

'I'm afraid not. I don't intend to put down any roots until I've decided what I want to do with my life.'

'Do I take it that you didn't go ahead with the wedding?' he said softly.

'No. I called it off that night, after I'd spoken to you.'

His eyes darkened with sympathy. 'It must have been very difficult for you.'

'It was.' She gave him a tight little smile, unwilling to go into detail when they were in such a public place. Thinking about the hurt she had caused everyone upset her and she didn't want to risk breaking down. 'I'd better go and read

Emily her story before she thinks I've forgotten about it,' she said, edging away.

'Of course. But if you ever need to talk, I'm a good listener, Heather. Remember that, won't you?'

'I shall. Thank you.'

Another smile and she made her escape. However, as she went back to the little girl's bed, Heather felt a new lightness in her spirit. For the past few weeks she had done nothing but berate herself for the mess she'd made of things and it was a relief not to feel guilty for a change.

She sighed because it would be stupid to get carried away by Archie's kindness. She had every reason to feel guilty when she had let so many people down. It hadn't been only Ross who'd been affected by her decision not to go ahead with the wedding, but both their families as well. Her father in particular had been terribly distressed. He seemed to believe that he was to blame in some way, but that wasn't true.

Matthew Thompson had done everything he could to make sure that Heather had been safe and happy since her mother had died so tragically after suffering a stroke. Heather had been fifteen at the time and she had been devastated by her mother's death. Her father had been, too, but he had focused all his energy on helping Heather come to terms with her loss.

It had brought them even closer so that Heather had had no hesitation about taking a job in Dalverston after she'd finished her nursing degree. Her father had supported her for all those years and she'd wanted to be there for him, too. Ross's mother had been a partner at the general practice her father had run for a number of years, and when Ross had completed his GP training, he had joined the practice as well.

It had been inevitable that she and Ross would end up spending time together and eventually they had drifted into a relationship. Both sets of parents had approved and Heather had taken it as a sign that they were meant to be together. It had only been as the wedding had drawn nearer that she'd started having doubts and even then she hadn't acted on them until it had been almost too late.

She had caused a lot of hurt and unhappiness for the people who loved her, and now she had to make up for it by learning to stand on her own two feet. Moving to London could turn out to be a mistake but it would be up to her to deal with it. No matter how kind Archie Carew had been to her, she wouldn't turn to him again for help.

CHAPTER THREE

IT WAS almost nine p.m. by the time Archie finally made it home and he was exhausted. Working fifteen hours straight was no joke, especially when it had been after midnight before he'd gone to bed the previous night. He went straight to the kitchen and raided the fridge. All he could find was a lump of slightly mouldy cheese and a tomato but it would have to do. He definitely wasn't heading out again to find himself something else to eat.

He made cheese on toast, slicing the tomato on the top so that he could ease his conscience by telling himself he was eating at least one of the requisite portions of fruit and veg he was supposed to consume each day. He ate in the kitchen because the dining-room table was piled up with cartons. He had been planning to do some more packing that night, but after he had finished his supper, he couldn't face it.

He made himself a cup of instant coffee and retired to the sitting room, glad that at least he had something to sit on. He had packed away all the ornaments and pictures so the room looked very bare but at least he had a seat. Slumping down on the sofa, he sipped his coffee, grimacing at the powdery aftertaste it left on his tongue. Although he was quite an accomplished cook, he never bothered cooking nowadays. There was no one to share a meal with and that took all the pleasure out of it.

The thought immediately reminded him of Stephanie and he sighed. He tried not to think about her too often but it wasn't easy. Before the accident his future had been all mapped out, and mapped out the way he had always dreamed it would be, too. He'd had a job he'd loved and a woman he'd wanted to spend his life with. He had been perfectly happy with his lot until his world had fallen apart.

Archie stood up, too restless to sit there while the thoughts ran like rats around his brain. Going over to the bureau, he opened a drawer and took out an old chocolate box. He had been meaning to sort through it for weeks but each time he'd put off doing it because it had been too painful. However, he was already upset so he may as well get it over with now.

He sat down and emptied the contents of the box onto the cushion beside him. There were dozens of photographs along with other mementoes of his life with Stephanie. He picked up a programme for the ballet, smiling ruefully as he recalled how angry Stephanie had been when he had fallen asleep during the performance. Next came a single ticket for the opera—he'd had to miss the show when he'd been called into work. Then there was an out-of-date train ticket for an aborted trip by Eurostar to Paris—Stephanie had gone by herself in the end as he'd been too busy.

Archie frowned as he continued to delve through the remnants of their life together. There'd been an awful lot of occasions when he had let Stephanie down. Work had always been his number one priority and everything else had come a poor second, including Stephanie. Was it any wonder, really, that she'd sought solace with someone else?

He picked up another photograph, feeling pain tug at his heart as he studied the smiling faces of the people in it. It had been taken a couple of years ago when he, Stephanie and his brother, Duncan, had spent some time together at the family estate in Scotland. Stephanie had stayed on when he'd had to return to London and he'd thought nothing of it at the time.

Now he couldn't help wondering if that had been when his fiancée had fallen in love with his brother, after he had abandoned her for the umpteenth time. It was one more reason to feel guilty, another reason why he needed to make amends for what he had done. If he had paid more attention to what had been going on around him, Stephanie and Duncan might not have died.

It was gone four in the morning when Charlie Maguire suffered a second heart attack. Heather grabbed the crash trolley and raced to his bed. Marion had already started CPR and she looked up when Heather appeared.

'Plug that in then phone the switchboard and ask them to page Mike. We need him back here, stat!'

'Will do.'

Heather flew to the phone and dialled the switchboard. 'It's Heather from Paeds,' she said as soon as the operator answered. 'Can you page Dr Mike Bridges, please? We need him here urgently.'

She hung up after the operator confirmed her request. Some of the other children had woken up now, disturbed by all the commotion, so she made her way around the ward, doing her best to settle them down. Marion and the other nurse on duty that night, Abby Connor, were working on Charlie, but it was a relief when the registrar arrived. He headed straight to the boy's bed, looking very grim when Marion explained what had happened.

'We'll shock him and see if that works. I'll need some adrenaline—can someone sort that out for me, please?'

'I'll do it,' Heather offered immediately.

Mike told her the dosage while Marion gave her the keys to the drugs trolley. When she got back, the team had defibrillated Charlie's heart once and were about to perform the procedure a second time because there was still no output.

Heather found herself willing the child to respond as the paddles were once again placed on his chest.

'Clear!' Mike rapped out.

Everyone held their breath as another charge of electricity shot through the boy's body, but there was still nothing on the monitor apart from a flat green line. Mike turned to her and she could see the worry on his face as he took the drugs from her.

'Get onto Archie. Tell him what's happened and that it's not looking good.'

'Of course,' Heather agreed, hiding her surprise because in her experience it wasn't usual to phone a consultant during the night.

She hurried to the phone again and found Archie's number listed with all the others. She keyed it in and waited anxiously for him to pick up. If anyone could help Charlie, it was Archie— he would know what to do in *any* crisis.

She bit her lip because she really shouldn't be

thinking along such lines. It would be only too easy to see Archie as her saviour as well and that wouldn't do. She cleared her throat when a sleepy male voice mumbled hello.

'I'm sorry to bother you, Mr Carew, but Mike Bridges asked me to phone you. Charlie Maguire has had a second myocardial infarction and we're having problems stabilising him.'

'How long ago did it happen?' he demanded, instantly alert. Heather had a quick mental flash of him dragging himself up out of bed and just as quickly dismissed it. She couldn't afford to get sidetracked.

'Roughly five minutes.'

'Right. I'm on my way. Tell Dr Bridges to continue CPR until I get there.'

'Yes, sir,' Heather replied, responding automatically to the authority in his voice.

'Thank you, Heather,' he said quietly before the line went dead.

Heather's hand was trembling as she gently

replaced the receiver on its rest. Although she hadn't introduced herself, Archie must have recognised her voice and it gave her a funny feeling inside to realise that. As she went to relay his message to the others, Heather found herself smiling before she realised how stupid she was being to set any store by it. Archie was only going to feature in her life for as long she worked here. He certainly wasn't going to play any part in her future.

'Is everyone agreed, then?'

Archie looked at the group assembled around Charlie Maguire's bed and saw the same expressions on their faces that must have been on his own. Despite all their efforts, they'd been unable to resuscitate the boy and his death had upset them all.

'Time of death 5:13,' he said when they all nodded. 'Thank you for everything you did. I'm only sorry it didn't work out in the end.'

He pushed the curtain aside, feeling despondency weighing down on him as he made his way to the office. Losing a child was always a heartbreaking experience but it had become even more difficult since Duncan and Stephanie had died. It was hard to accept that so many lives should be cut short far too soon.

Heather was in the office; she looked up when he went in and he saw her expression change when he shook his head. 'I'm so sorry,' she said, her voice catching, and Archie had to swallow when he felt a lump come to his throat. He could tell that she'd truly meant what she'd said and that it hadn't been just a polite expression of regret. It touched him deeply, far more deeply than it should have done, in fact.

'We all are,' he said shortly, because breaking down wasn't an option. 'Have the parents arrived yet?'

'Yes. They're in the relatives' room.' She was

all business once more and Archie was suddenly sorry that he had been so short with her.

'Right. I'll have a word with them, then.' He turned to the door, stopped, walked another step, then swung round. 'Look, I didn't mean to snap at you, but it always hits me hard whenever we lose a child.'

He gave her a tight smile, wondering why he felt that he had to explain himself. He wouldn't have done so under normal circumstances, yet for some reason he didn't want Heather to get the wrong idea. 'I can't afford to get too emotional when I need to speak to Charlie's family.'

'I understand.' Her eyes filled with compassion as she looked at him. 'I don't think it's possible to do this job unless you care, but it's hard, isn't it, when something like this happens? It makes you remember the people you have lost, too.'

'It does,' he said quietly, then left before he was tempted to say anything else. It seemed his suspicions had been correct. However, he knew that asking Heather whom she had lost would be a mistake at the moment. It would only lead to him telling her about Duncan and he didn't think he could cope with that right now.

He made his way to the relatives' room and spoke to the boy's parents. It was every bit as bad as he had expected and he was emotionally wrung out after he finished. He made sure the parents knew that they could sit with Charlie for as long as they wanted to, then asked Marion to escort them to a side room. Charlie would be taken there from the ward so the family could have some privacy. Sorting out such details was all part and parcel of his job, but it was so much more than mere routine and he would never be able to treat it as such. Mind you, he wouldn't have to after he returned to Scotland. Maybe that was the plus side of giving up his job?

He tried to put a positive spin on the thought but he was all out of optimism. The cloud of gloom that had been hanging over him seemed to intensify as he went back to the ward and had a word with Mike, who was equally despondent. Archie assured him that he had done everything he could, but he knew his registrar didn't believe him and that Mike wouldn't have been half the doctor he was if he had done. As Heather had said, you had to care otherwise you couldn't do this job properly.

As though thinking about her had conjured her up, she suddenly appeared. It was just gone six a.m. and she was on her way home. Archie frowned as he watched her button up her coat as she hurried along the corridor. Was that it, then? Was she going to leave and disappear for good? He had no idea if she was booked to work at the hospital again. Some agency staff did full weeks, others preferred to do the odd session here and there, and he had no idea which category she fell into. However, the thought that she might walk out of the door and that would be the last he saw her of her was very hard to swallow.

Archie wasn't sure what his intentions were when he found himself following her. He wasn't even sure if it was a good idea but that didn't stop him. He put on a spurt when he saw her get into the lift but the doors closed before he could reach it.

He took the stairs instead, two at a time, careering down them as though a pack of hungry hounds was snapping at his heels. Heather was already leaving the building by the time he exited the stairwell so he raced after her, then had to stop when he reached the main door to let an elderly woman pass through ahead of him. He helped the old lady manoeuvre her walking frame inside then set off again—down the steps, across the car park, out into the street…

He ground to a halt when he spotted Heather standing at the bus stop. Quite frankly, he wasn't sure what came next. Should he go over and tell her that he would like to see her again, maybe even ask her out? Bearing in mind recent events, did he really think she would accept?

Archie groaned when he realised how stupid it was to imagine that Heather might be interested in seeing him again. She had just run out on her wedding and going out with him would be the last thing on her mind!

It should have been the last thing on his mind, too. In a few weeks' time he would be moving to Scotland and he would have enough on his plate, learning how to run the estate. He'd never taken much interest in it before—that had been Duncan's prerogative. As the elder son, Duncan had always known that he would become Laird one day and had planned his life accordingly. Whereas some people might have felt aggrieved that they would never inherit either the title or the land, Archie had felt relieved. It had meant that he could follow his dream and become a doctor, but all that had changed on Duncan's death. Now he was Laird and he had responsibilities to go with the title. He would be far too busy in the coming months to take on anything else.

He was still chewing it all over when Heather suddenly glanced round and spotted him. In that instant he knew that, no matter how crazy it was, he couldn't let her get on the bus and disappear from his life for good. He would be constantly wondering what had happened to her and he couldn't bear it.

He made his way over to her, feeling his insides judder when she gave him a tentative smile. Despite the busy night, she looked so beautiful as she stood there in the grey morning light that he'd have needed a heart of stone not to be aware of it. It was an effort to remember that neither of them was in a position to go looking for romance and behave accordingly.

'Hi. I spotted you leaving and wondered if you fancied having breakfast with me.' He pointed across the road. 'The café over there does the best breakfasts in London. Can I tempt you?'

CHAPTER FOUR

'THANK you.'

Heather waited while the waitress arranged her cutlery in front of her. She still wasn't sure why she had accepted Archie's invitation. After all, what was the point of spending any time with him? Although she had agreed to work at the hospital for the next few weeks, she wouldn't stay on after that. It would be silly to get involved with him when there was no future for them.

She drew herself up short. Archie had offered to buy her breakfast, not suggest they should have an affair! Colour rushed to her face and she snatched up her cup of coffee to hide her discomfort.

'Hmm. You can't beat a decent cup of coffee.' Archie inhaled deeply as he savoured the aroma, then grinned at her. 'This is the point where I should really stand up and confess.'

'Confess,' Heather repeated blankly.

'Uh-huh.' He pushed back his chair and stood up. There was a smile twitching the corners of his mouth as he recited solemnly, 'My name is Archie and I'm a coffee addict.'

Heather chuckled, appreciating the fact that he could make fun of himself that way. 'Your secret is safe. There's just me and a couple of dozen other people in here who've witnessed your confession.'

'That's all right, then.' He resumed his seat and smiled at her. 'It was worth outing myself just to hear you laugh.'

Heather sighed. 'There hasn't been much to laugh about recently.'

'I can imagine. Life must have been pretty difficult for you these past couple of months.'

'It has.' She shrugged, wondering how much she should tell him. It was her problem and she had to deal with it herself. However, the thought of being able to share some of the heartache with him was too tempting to resist. 'I hurt a lot of people and it isn't easy to deal with that thought.'

'Have you made your peace with your ex-fiancé?' he enquired, his green eyes filling with sympathy.

'Not really.' Heather grimaced as she felt a wave of guilt rise up inside her. 'I haven't actually spoken to Ross yet. I know I should have done, but I had no idea what to say to him. I sent him a letter, apologising for what I was doing, but it really wasn't enough. I'll have to speak to him at some point and I can only hope he'll forgive me.'

'I imagine he's had time to think things through by now and realised you made the right decision.' Archie shrugged when she looked at him in surprise. 'I can't believe he didn't know that something wasn't right. His gut instinct must have told him that you weren't happy.'

'I don't know about that. Ross isn't big on following his instincts. He's always very much in control—knows exactly what he wants from life and goes for it.' She shook her head when she realised how that may have sounded. 'That wasn't meant as a criticism. Ross is just very single-minded and doesn't allow anything to stand in his way. It's one of the things I've always admired about him, in fact.'

'Do you think he'll find it hard to accept that you changed your mind about marrying him?'

'I suppose the truthful answer is that I don't know. I can't see him falling apart, though, if that's what you mean. It just isn't in his nature.' She sighed. 'My father will have a harder time accepting what's happened. He was terribly upset, blamed himself for pushing me and Ross together. He wouldn't listen when I tried to explain that it was my fault, not his.'

Tears welled in her eyes and Archie reached across the table and squeezed her hand. 'I'm sure your father will get over it in time, Heather.'

'I hope so.'

Fortunately, their breakfast arrived just then. Heather had opted for scrambled eggs on toast but Archie had ordered the full works—bacon, eggs, sausages, tomatoes, mushrooms, fried bread—and he tucked in with relish.

'Hungry?' Heather said drolly, scooping up a forkful of buttery eggs.

'Ravenous.' He popped a chunk of sausage into his mouth, chewed and swallowed, then smiled at her. 'The only thing left in the fridge last night was a lump of cheese and a tomato so supper wasn't exactly a cordon bleu experience.'

'Don't tell me that you're one of those men who can't tell a frying pan from a Frisbee,' she accused him, picking up a triangle of toast.

'The frying pan's the one with the handle, isn't it?' he replied with a wicked little chuckle.

Heather felt her heart give the oddest little leap and hastily averted her eyes from his laughing face. For some reason she felt all jittery inside and she couldn't understand it. She bit off a corner of toast then stole a glance at him, feeling shock ripple along her veins when she realised all of a sudden how good-looking he was. She hadn't paid much attention to how Archie looked before, mainly because she'd had other things on her mind, but suddenly she was seeing him as a man, and a very attractive one, too.

Facts tumbled over themselves as her brain rushed to log them. He was tall, over six feet, and well built, too, with a muscular chest and broad shoulders. His face was craggy rather than conventionally handsome, his features very masculine with those strong, uncompromising lines. His eyes were gorgeous, a clear deep green framed by dark brown lashes. His hair was the same rich brown colour, thick and glossy as it fell across his forehead. A mouth that had a tendency to curl upwards at the slightest excuse completed the picture. All things considered, Archie Carew was a man whom any woman would be happy to be seen with, and she was no exception.

Heather took a quick little breath as that thought wriggled its way into her head. She was happy to be there with Archie, very happy indeed.

Archie wasn't sure what Heather was thinking as she stared at him across the table. He cleared his throat, uncomfortable at finding himself on the end of such an intent scrutiny, and saw her jump. There was a touch of colour in her cheeks as she applied herself to her breakfast that intrigued him, although he wasn't going to make the mistake of asking her what was wrong. He didn't want to make her feel uncomfortable.

The need he felt to protect her surprised him. Although he tried to make allowances for other people's feelings, he didn't usually tiptoe around them. If he wanted an answer, he asked the question, but it was different with Heather. She was so vulnerable at the moment and he was very aware how easy it would be to hurt her, and that was something he wanted to avoid.

He followed her lead and concentrated on his meal, mopping the last eggy bits off his plate with a chunk of bread speared on the end of his fork. Placing his cutlery neatly on his plate, he sat back and sighed. 'That was delicious.'

'It was. Thank you.'

Heather popped the last morsel of toast into her mouth then licked her lips. Archie felt his stomach muscles clench as he watched the tip of her tongue slide seductively around her mouth. He wasn't normally given to fantasies of a sexual nature, but he was having the devil of a job to stop himself fantasising now. Imagining how it would feel if *his* tongue did that to her lips was giving him hot and cold chills!

Thankfully, Heather seemed oblivious to his dilemma. She wiped her fingers on a paper napkin and smiled at him. 'I'll definitely come here again. I've not had time to find any decent places to eat since I moved to London. Most of the restaurants are far too pricey for my budget.'

'How long have you been here?' Archie asked, determined to get himself back on the straight and narrow.

'Almost three months.'

'That long?' His brows rose steeply. 'You must have come down here straight after I saw you.'

'That's right. I needed to get away so I caught the train that very night.'

'I see. Did you live in Dalverston or was that just where you were getting married?' he asked, curious to find out more about her.

'I lived there. I was born there, in fact.' She gave a little shrug. 'My dad's the local GP and he has a practice in the town. It started out as a one-man operation but it's expanded in recent years. There are five doctors working there now, including Ross and his mother, Rachel.'

Archie whistled. 'A real family affair from the sound of it. What about you? Did you work at the practice too?'

'No, at the local hospital, Dalverston General. I was a staff nurse on the paediatric ward.' Her face clouded. 'It was a wrench to leave but I thought it was the best thing to do in the circumstances. I didn't want people continually asking me why Ross and I hadn't got married so I decided to move to London where nobody knew me.'

'They say a change is as good as a rest,' Archie observed, deliberately lightening the mood because he couldn't bear to see her looking so unhappy.

'So they do.' She summoned a smile. 'How about you? You're not from London, are you?'

'No. I grew up in Scotland, although I spent a fair bit of time at boarding school in England.'

'Is that why you moved here to work?'

'Not really. It just happened that a post came up in London and I ended up here.'

'Would you like to go back to Scotland one day?' she asked, obviously interested.

'I'm going back there at the end of this month, actually.'

'Really?'

'Yes. My older brother, Duncan, was killed last year in a car crash and I'm going home to take over the running of the family estate.'

'You mean that you're taking a job in Scotland so you can oversee the running of the estate,' she queried, but Archie shook his head.

'No. I mean that I'm giving up medicine.' He could feel his heart sink at the thought and hurried on. He knew what he had to do, and why. It was his penance for causing the death of two people he had loved.

'The estate is far too big for me to run it on a part-time basis. Something had to give and in the end it was my job.' He glanced at his watch, checked the date and shrugged. 'I'm working out my notice at the moment, but in a few weeks I shall be on my way.'

'Is it what you really want?' She leant forward and he could see the doubt in her eyes. 'Giving up your career is a huge step to take, surely?'

'It's what I have to do,' he said quietly. 'There are several hundred people working on the estate and I'm responsible for their welfare.'

'But couldn't you hire someone to do the job for you, some sort of manager who would deal with the everyday affairs?'

'I've tried that. I hired a factor to run the estate after Duncan died but it hasn't worked out. There's been a lot of problems and the business has suffered. Duncan devoted his life to making sure the estate was successful when he took it over after our father died. It isn't fair to his memory or to the people who rely on the estate for their livelihood if I let it go to rack and ruin.'

'It must have been very hard for you, though. Losing your brother would have been difficult enough, but to have to give up your career as well...' She trailed off and Archie sighed.

'It has been hard. I put off making the decision for months. It was only when I went up there a few months ago and saw for myself what had been happening that I realised I had to do something.'

'Was that where you'd been before you arrived in Dalverston?'

'Yes. I was driving down from Scotland and decided to break my journey and spend the night there.'

'And ended up helping me.' She reached across the table and touched his hand. 'Thank you. The kindness you showed me that day helped me enormously.'

'I'm glad.'

Archie picked up his cup for the simple reason that if he didn't move his hand out of the way, he would be tempted to cling to her, and that was the last thing he should do. He finished his coffee and asked the waitress for the bill. Heather thanked him politely for buying her breakfast, although her face was unusually grave as she looked at him.

'The agency has asked me to work at the hospital for a few weeks—is that all right with you? I can tell them I've changed my mind if you think it will create a problem.'

Archie shook his head, trying to disguise his relief at the thought that he would see her again. 'Of course it isn't a problem, Heather. I'm more than happy to work with you.'

'That's all right, then.' She gave him a quick smile as she stood up. 'Thank you again for breakfast and everything else. I hope that things work out for you in the future.'

'You, too,' he said with a smile that felt as though it had been dredged up from his boots. Heather may be willing to work with him, but she'd made it clear that she wouldn't be seeking him out for any more cosy little chats across the breakfast table.

It was no more than he could have expected, yet he couldn't deny that he felt decidedly out of sorts as they left the café. Heather bid him a hasty goodbye when she spotted her bus coming along the street and he didn't try to detain her. There was no point. They'd done the whole 'thanks for your help, you're welcome' routine, so now they could carry on and work together, untroubled by what had gone on before.

Archie knew he should be pleased that they'd sorted everything out. After all, he wasn't looking for another relationship. He'd learned his lesson from what had happened with Stephanie. Sometimes it felt as though he was jinxed. Everyone he had ever loved had died and he was terrified of it happening again. He didn't think he could bear to let himself get close to someone else and lose that person, too. It was far better to accept that he and Heather would never be anything more than colleagues.

Heather found it difficult to sleep after she returned home to the small basement flat she rented in Putney. Sleeping during the day was always difficult, and especially in the city where there was so much noise. However, it was less the sound of the traffic than her own thoughts that was causing a problem that day. After a couple of hours spent tossing and turning, she got up and made herself a cup of tea. She took it into the sitting room and sat down on the lumpy old sofa, thinking back over everything that had happened that morning.

She had really enjoyed talking to Archie. It had been the longest conversation she'd had since she'd arrived in London, in fact. However, it wasn't loneliness that had made the experience seem like such a highlight, but Archie himself. There was something about him that she responded to.

She smiled as she recalled the way he had stood up and declared himself a coffee addict. He had a wonderfully droll sense of humour and didn't seem to feel that he had to stand on his dignity despite his position. She'd worked with a lot of consultants and some of them had been extremely pompous, but not Archie.

The fact that he was brilliant at his job was another thing she admired about him. He obviously cared deeply about the children he treated, and was willing to go the extra mile to help them. It made his decision to give up his career all the more shocking.

Heather frowned. She had a feeling there was more to his decision than he had admitted. Although she appreciated why he was concerned about the future of the estate, giving up his career seemed such a drastic step to take. It was almost as though he felt under pressure to step into his brother's shoes and she couldn't help wondering why. Had something happened that had made Archie feel he was obligated to take on the job?

It was impossible to work out what could have caused Archie to feel that way and in the end she gave up. She decided to go to the supermarket to save her having to go at the weekend. She had agreed to work permanent nights for the next few weeks because the agency had offered her extra money and she needed every penny. Although her father had refused to accept the cheque she had offered him as recompense for the cost of her cancelled wedding, she had no intention of touching the money herself.

It wasn't fair that her father should have to bear the financial loss as well as the emotional upset so she would manage on what she earned. If it wasn't enough for her to live in London, she would move somewhere else. It wasn't as though there was anything to keep her in the city. All her friends lived in Dalverston and she'd not had time to make any new ones, apart from Archie, and he was leaving at the end of the month.

Heather bit her lip when she felt a twinge of disappointment run through her. She knew it was silly, but she was going to miss Archie. Even in the short time she'd known him, he seemed to have carved out a niche for himself in her life.

CHAPTER FIVE

THE week wore on, the usual mix of high drama and the mundane. The paediatric unit was a busy place to work and Archie found himself staying on most evenings way after the time he should have finished. He didn't mind, though. It gave him a chance to see Heather, and that more than made up for the extra time he spent at work.

It appeared that Heather had been hired to work nights for the whole of the time she was due to cover at the hospital. Archie was surprised when he found that out because the agency staff usually chose their shifts to suit themselves. He mentioned it to Wendy on Thursday afternoon and she nodded.

'I thought it was unusual, too, but Heather told me the agency couldn't find anyone else to cover. Night shifts are never popular and a lot of nurses won't work them if they don't have to do so.'

'I'm surprised that Heather was willing to do three full weeks of nights,' Archie observed.

'She said she needed the money. The agency pays extra for night work and that was the incentive, apparently.'

Wendy changed the subject and started to tell him about a child who'd been admitted that morning with an incisional hernia. Archie forced himself to concentrate while they discussed the case, but as soon as Wendy finished, his mind returned to Heather and the reason why she was short of money. Living in London was extremely costly and a nurse's salary wouldn't go very far. However, he hated to think that she might be struggling financially and decided to have a word with her as soon as he got the chance.

The opportunity arose not long after she came on duty that evening. The child with the hernia, a seven-year-old boy called Kojo Arutee, had been creating a fuss ever since he'd been admitted. Archie knew that the staff had been struggling to keep Kojo under control all afternoon, and once the boy realised there were different nurses on duty, his be-haviour rapidly deteriorated. Archie was checking another child's obs when he heard a crash and, looking round, discovered that Kojo had overturned a trolley of drinks. Heather was in the process of trying to clear every-thing up as well as stop Kojo from causing any more damage.

Archie strode straight over to them and bent down so that he and Kojo were on eye level. 'This has to stop, Kojo. I'm not letting you run riot in here and disturb all the other children.'

Kojo didn't say a word as he picked up a cup of milk and emptied it onto the floor. Archie shook his head. 'No. If you can't behave properly then you can't stay here. Is that what you want, to have to go home with that horrible bulge still sticking out of your tummy?'

The little boy considered that then shook his head. Archie turned to Heather. 'If Kojo says he's sorry and helps you clear up, can he stay and have his operation?'

'Yes, so long as he promises to be a good boy from now on,' Heather said with a smile that made Archie's heart leap in his chest.

He battened it down into its rightful place as he turned to the little boy, hoping that Heather couldn't tell the effect she'd had on him. 'It's up to you, Kojo. What are you going to do?'

'Be a good boy,' the child recited solemnly.

'Good.' Archie ruffled his wiry black curls. 'Now, how about picking up all those spoons and taking them into the kitchen so they can be washed?'

Kojo immediately bent down and gathered

up the teaspoons. He trotted off down the ward and disappeared into the kitchen with them. Heather laughed.

'I wouldn't have believed it if I hadn't seen it for myself. How did you know he'd respond to your threats to send him home?'

'A lucky guess.' Archie smiled when she pulled a face. 'No, honestly, it was. I'm only glad it did the trick. We can do without that kind of distraction.'

'We certainly can.'

She bent down to right the trolley, nodding her thanks when he helped her set it back on its wheels. Fortunately, they used plastic beakers in the ward so there was no broken glass to clear up, just the spilled milk and the juice. Heather manoeuvred the trolley out of the way.

'I'll just mop this up then everything will be as good as new,' she told him, heading off down the ward.

Archie followed her, wondering if this was

the right moment to mention her finances. He didn't want it to appear as though he was interfering but he hated to think that she might be having trouble paying her bills.

'I believe you're working permanent nights here,' he said as he watched her take a mop and bucket out of the cleaner's cupboard.

'That's right. The agency had problems finding anyone willing to work nights so I said I'd do them.'

'Wendy said that you told her you needed the extra money?'

'Yes. It will come in very handy.'

She took the bucket into the sluice room and turned on the tap, looking round in surprise when Archie followed her in. He shrugged, wondering how best to broach the subject.

'If money is tight at the moment, Heather, I'd be happy to help any way I can.'

'Thank you but I can manage,' she said shortly, lifting the bucket out of the sink. She went to step around him and he sighed when he saw the mutinous set to her mouth.

'Now I've upset you and that was the last thing I meant to do. I'm sorry.'

'No, it's me who should apologise.' She put the bucket on the floor and grimaced. 'It's kind of you to offer, Archie, but I can't take your money. Quite apart from the fact that it would be wrong to play on your kindness, I need to stand on my own two feet.'

'Everyone needs a helping hand from time to time,' he said softly. 'That's all it would be—a helping hand. There definitely wouldn't be any strings attached to the offer, if that's what worries you,' he added in case she'd got the wrong idea.

A little heat touched her cheeks. 'I never imagined there would be. I'd just feel very uncomfortable about taking money from you. You do understand, I hope.'

'Of course. But if you change your mind, the offer still stands. OK?'

'Yes. Thanks, Archie. I appreciate it.'

She disappeared out of the door, leaving him wondering what else he could have said to persuade her. He sighed because it wouldn't have been right to force her to accept his offer just so he would feel better. It was up to Heather how she chose to run her life, and he had no say in the matter. It was a good job, too, bearing in mind what had happened to Stephanie and Duncan. The least amount of input he had in Heather's affairs, the safer she would be.

Heather worked straight through until ten p.m. then went to the canteen for her break. There were just two of them on duty that night so they had to take their breaks separately, not that she minded. It was often difficult to make conversation with the full-time staff. Some weren't interested in making friends with agency workers and others were indifferent. It was easier just to do her job.

The kitchen closed at six p.m. so the choice was limited to sandwiches or microwave snacks. She opted for some egg and cress sandwiches, added a chocolate bar for dessert and a cup of tea, then paid for her meal. It wasn't very busy in the canteen so she had her choice of tables and chose one by the window that gave her a view over the city.

It was really spectacular at night when everywhere was lit up. She could see Big Ben and the Houses of Parliament, with the London Eye on the opposite bank of the Thames. It all looked so glamorous and cosmopolitan compared to the rural charms of Dalverston that she felt a ripple of excitement run through her. She was living and working in the most exciting city in the world, and she should be making the most of the opportunity.

Fired up by enthusiasm, she drank in the view while she ate her supper. Since she had arrived in London, she had been dwelling on the negative aspects of the move but it was time that changed. This was a new beginning for her, not just a means to escape from the past. She could go anywhere she wanted, even move abroad if that's what she chose to do.

Although she would miss her father, he needed to think about himself for a change. He had put his life on hold after her mother had died and he deserved to find happiness again. Now that she had struck out on her own, there was nothing to stop him. There was nothing to stop her either. The world was her oyster and there was nothing to keep her in England…except Archie.

Heather frowned as that thought slid into her mind. It felt so right, so *normal*, to factor Archie into the equation, yet she couldn't understand why. She didn't owe Archie anything, but she couldn't deny that the thought of moving to the other side of the world and never seeing him again was unsettling.

Why? Was it the fact that Archie was such a

good listener that made her feel this way? she wondered. He was kind and sympathetic, and he seemed to understand her concerns, so was it any wonder that she felt so close to him?

Heather heaved a sigh of relief, glad that she had managed to make sense of it all. Archie's kindness was just what she needed at this difficult time and there was no need to worry. It definitely couldn't be anything else. Not at the moment. She wouldn't be that stupid. She had just ended one relationship and there was no way that she was going to do something really crazy like fall in love with Archie!

It was gone midnight before Archie went to bed that night after another mammoth session of packing. His flat was starting to resemble a storage unit with all the boxes piled up in every room. Everything needed to be ready in time for the move and there was no one else he trusted to sort out his belongings. Nevertheless, he had to admit that packing away his life into a pile of cardboard boxes was making him feel increasingly dejected.

His mood didn't improve the following morning either. He had an early clinic at eight and when he arrived at the outpatients department he discovered the computers were down. His list was already long and the fact that he would need to physically delve through each patient's file rather than pick out key points on the computer would increase the amount of time it took. By the time ten o'clock came around he was only a third of the way down the list. Jackie Bliss, the senior outpatient nurse, was assisting him; she rolled her eyes as she handed him yet another set of case notes.

'Timothy Wray, aged eleven. His family has just moved here from the south coast. Tim was seen by his GP on several occasions but nothing definite was found. He's been complaining of headaches and severe pain in and around his left ear.'

'Did the GP refer him to a dentist?' Archie asked, opening the file.

'Yes, but the dentist couldn't find anything wrong with his teeth that might have caused the problem,' Jackie replied promptly.

'I see.' Archie nodded, appreciating the fact that Jackie had saved him having to find the dental report. He skimmed through the case history, taking note of the fact that Tim had been extremely healthy until recently. He'd had the usual childhood ailments but nothing serious. 'I take it that Tim hasn't seen a consultant on the south coast?'

'No. The family was about to move to London so the GP decided to refer him straight to us.' Jackie went to the door. 'Shall I call him in?'

'Yep, you may as well.'

Archie quickly read through the rest of the patient's history but there was nothing there that indicated why Tim had been suffering such symptoms. He stood up when Jackie ushered the boy and his mother into the room.

'Hello. My name's Archie Carew. I'm the consultant in charge of the paediatric unit.' He shook the mother's hand then smiled at the boy. 'You must be Tim.'

'That's right.' Tim didn't appear at all nervous as he sat down by the desk. He stared around the room, his eyes widening when he spotted the skeleton standing in the corner. 'Wow! Is that thing real?'

'It is.' Archie got up again. Picking up the stand, he placed the skeleton beside his desk. 'Fred and I go back a long way. I bought him when I was at med school studying to be a doctor and we got into a lot of scrapes together.'

'Cool!' Tim murmured. 'Can I touch him?'

'Of course you can. Here, you can shake his hand.' Archie took hold of the skeleton by the right ulna and radius and held out its hand. Tim laughed when the metacarpal bones and phalanges tinkled merrily as he shook it.

'That's wicked! I wish I had one.'

'Something to put on next year's Christmas list,' Archie suggested, drolly. He sat down, pleased that they had broken the ice. The key to treating a child was to form a bond with him, as he'd done with Tim. He smiled at Mrs Wray, hoping to put her at her ease, too. 'Now that you've met old Fred, why don't you tell me how Tim has been recently?'

'Just the same, Dr Carew. He gets these horrible headaches and his face hurts.'

Archie didn't correct her by pointing out that as a consultant his correct title should have been Mr Carew. It was immaterial to him what people called him and most were more comfortable with the title of Doctor. 'I see. Can you tell me when this all started? It's not clear from the referral letter if this has been going on for some time or if it's a fairly recent event.'

'It started last autumn, not long after Tim went back to school after the summer holidays,' Mrs Wray explained.

'And had anything happened before then?' Archie probed.

'I'm not sure what you mean, Doctor.'

'Had Tim been ill or maybe had an accident—something like that?'

'No, not that I can remember…'

'Dad had that crash in his car,' Tim said suddenly, interrupting them.

Archie turned to him, immediately on the alert. 'Were you in the car at the time?'

'Oh, yes. Dad was taking me to play football when this van ran into the back of us. It dented all the boot of our car and Dad was furious.'

'I bet he was.' Archie agreed thoughtfully. 'Did the headaches start after the accident?'

'About a week later. My neck was really sore, too.'

'Did your father take you to the hospital to be checked over?'

'No. Dad said there was no point 'cos we were both OK.'

Archie nodded. 'I see. So apart from the head-aches and the pain around your ear, is there anything else, Tim? Does your jaw feel sore when you chew, or does it click when you open your mouth wide?'

'Yes. And if I yawn it sort of locks and I can't shut it.'

'Do you think it's linked to the accident?' Mrs Wray asked anxiously.

'It could be.' Archie stood up and moved round to the front of the skeleton. He pointed to its jaw. 'The head of the mandible, or jawbone, fits into this hollow here on the underside of the temporal bone of the skull. In a living person there's a couple of strong muscles as well which work together to enable us to move the jaw when we're chewing food, for instance. However, if the joint has become misaligned, it causes pain and discomfort.'

'And you think it may have happened when

Derek and Tim had that accident?' Mrs Wray said slowly.

'I'd say it's extremely likely. Temporomandibular joint syndrome—which is basically what Tim has—can result if the head, the neck or the jaw are injured.' He went back to his desk. 'If Tim suffered even mild whiplash in the accident, it could have been enough to cause the problem.'

Mrs Wray shook her head. 'I should have guessed it had something to do with that accident. I feel so stupid for not mentioning it to our GP.'

'Don't blame yourself. It wasn't something you could have foreseen.' He took out a form and filled in Tim's details then passed it across the desk. 'I'd like Tim to have an X-ray. If it shows that the joint has been displaced then we'll know my diagnosis is correct.'

'And if it is, what will happen?' Mrs Wray asked.

'We might be able to manoeuvre the joint back into its proper place, or it might need a small operation to sort everything out.' He smiled reassuringly when he saw her pale. 'It's really nothing to worry about, Mrs Wray. Tim would just need to stay in hospital overnight if it does come down to an op. I'm sure you can cope with that, can't you, Tim?'

'Sure,' the boy agreed, unfazed by the idea.

Archie saw them out, wishing that all his young patients were as amenable as Tim, when he heard the sound of screaming coming from the waiting room. He asked Jackie to fetch the child in rather than risk him upsetting the rest of the children. He didn't want anything else to delay him otherwise he would never catch up and he would end up having to stay late again that evening.

Just for a moment the thought of seeing Heather again danced before his eyes before he blanked it out. No matter how alluring the prospect might be, he intended to leave on time that night. It was the only way he was going to stick to his decision not to get involved with her.

CHAPTER SIX

HEATHER hadn't intended to arrive so early for work that night but it just so happened that a bus came along as soon as she reached the stop. It whizzed through the traffic so that by the time she reached the hospital she had half an hour to spare. She decided to make the most of it and headed to the café. It was busy in there but there was an empty table in the corner so she sat down. The waitress had just brought her order when Archie came in.

Heather bit her lip when she saw him look around for a seat. Discovering that Archie had become a factor in any decisions she made about the future had left her feeling very uneasy. It was far too soon to get involved in another relationship. She simply couldn't trust her feelings at the moment so she had made up her mind to avoid Archie as much as she could. However, she couldn't pretend that she hadn't seen him when it would mean him having to wait for a seat.

Lifting her hand, she waved to him, feeling her heart jerk when she saw the surprise on his face. Just for a moment she thought he was going to ignore her, but then he waved back and she realised how ridiculous it was to imagine Archie would have done that. Just because she was attracted to him, it didn't mean he felt the same about her.

'This is a surprise. What are you doing here?'

He smiled as he stopped beside her table and Heather hastily smoothed her features into a suitably noncommittal expression. Allowing herself to feel disappointed because Archie wasn't as aware of her as she was of him was just plain crazy.

'My bus was early so I decided to have a quick cuppa before I signed in,' she explained, picking up the teapot.

'Good idea.' He pulled out a chair and sat down. 'I managed to get an early finish for once so I thought I'd have something to eat before I went home. Driving through London on a Friday night is a nightmare. I try to avoid it whenever possible.'

'I don't blame you.' Heather poured herself a cup of tea. 'Where do you live?'

'Chelsea.'

He caught the waitress's eye and beckoned her over. Heather turned over the other cup and filled it with tea while he placed his order.

'You shouldn't have done that,' he admonished her. 'That's your tea. I could have waited until mine arrived.'

'We may as well share it,' she told him lightly, not wanting to make an issue of it. 'I can always have a top-up when yours arrives.'

'Of course you can. Thanks.' He added a dash of milk and a couple of spoons of sugar then took a sip. 'Hmm, nearly as good as that coffee I had the other day.'

'Lucky it's only *nearly* as good,' she said tartly. 'At least you won't have to stand up and admit you're a tea addict as well.'

'No.' He glanced over his shoulder and chuckled. 'There's a few too many people in here at the moment to relish confessing my sins.'

'If your only sin is an addiction to coffee, you're not doing too badly.'

His face abruptly closed up. 'I wish it were my only sin.'

Heather had no idea what he meant, but it seemed that her comment had touched a nerve. She glanced at him and felt her heart ache when she saw the shadows in his eyes. It was obvious that something was troubling him, although she wasn't sure if it would be right to ask him what was wrong. In the end prudence won over emotion. Picking up the plate, she offered it to him.

'Would you like half of this scone to tide you over?'

'Thanks, but I'll wait for my meal.' He seemed to make an effort to shake off the aura of sadness as he smiled at her. 'So what did you get up to today?'

'Oh, nothing very much apart from catching up on some sleep.' She bit into the scone, clamping down on the idea that she might be able to make him feel better. Why on earth did she imagine that anything she did would cheer him up?

'It's always difficult to sleep through the day,' she continued, not wanting to dwell on that thought. 'Especially in the city. The traffic here never seems to stop.'

'Tell me about it. It used to drive me mad when I first moved here. I longed for some-where quiet where I couldn't hear the constant drone.' He shrugged. 'I'm used to it now and don't notice it as much. I imagine the same thing will happen to you.'

'If I stay here,' she amended, because it wasn't a foregone conclusion that she would remain in London. She intended to remain open to any new ideas, go with the flow and see where it took her.

'It sounds as though you're thinking about moving on.'

'I've not made up my mind what I'm going to do yet, to be honest.' She shrugged. 'I'm even toying with the idea of moving abroad. After all, there's nothing to keep me in England.'

'Footloose and fancy-free,' he said, smiling at her, and she smiled back when she saw that the spark was back in his eyes.

'That's me!'

They both laughed, both held eye contact a little longer than was necessary, and both dropped their gaze. Heather felt a fizz of aware-ness run through her. There was definitely something going on, something that Archie felt as well as she did, but would it be right to act on it? She really didn't need any more complications in her life at this stage. It was difficult enough to decide what to do without confusing the issue even more. Every decision she had ever made had been influenced by other people's expectations of her. From her parents to Ross, she had consciously, or unconsciously, factored in their views. Now it was time for her to be independent, her own woman. She needed to work out what she wanted from life and go for it. It would be downright silly for her and Archie to get involved right now.

Archie could feel his head buzzing. The way Heather was looking at him made it difficult for him to think straight. He longed to know what was going through her mind but doubted if he would make much sense of the answer even if he asked her. It was a relief when the waitress appeared with his meal and provided a much-needed distraction.

'That looks good.' Heather leant across the table and sniffed appreciatively. 'It smells good, too.'

'Want to share?' Archie offered, glad to have something tangible to focus on.

'I'd better not.' She glanced at her watch. 'Much as I would love to help you demolish those chips, I'd better get to work.'

'Another time, eh?' Archie said, cutting off a chunk of steak. He popped it into his mouth, hoping the protein would galvanise his over-loaded brain cells. It was ridiculous to wish that he and Heather could get to know each other better. Soon he would be leaving London and moving to the opposite end of the country. It wasn't the right time to start a relationship, and certainly not with Heather. Heather needed time to adjust to her newly single status and decide if it was really what she wanted. Although she claimed she'd done the right thing by not going ahead with the wedding, she must still have feelings for her ex.

As for him, well, he had no idea how he felt, if he was honest. Was he over Stephanie? Would he *ever* get over her? At one point it had seemed inconceivable that he would recover from the pain of discovering that the woman he had loved had been in love with his brother, but how did he feel about it now?

'We'll see.'

Heather gave him a noncommittal smile as she finished the last of her tea. Archie wasn't sure what it was about the smile that got to him, but all of a sudden he was tired of being sensible. Maybe he didn't know how he felt about Stephanie, but he knew that he wanted to spend more time with Heather. Surely there was no harm in asking her out so long as they kept things on a strictly platonic footing?

'What are you doing at the weekend, apart from sleeping?' he said hurriedly as she put down her cup.

'I haven't really thought about it. Why?'

'I was just wondering if you fancied going out somewhere,' he said, aiming for nonchalance and missing it by a mile. It was one thing to tell himself there was no harm in seeing Heather so long as it was on a purely friendly basis, but it was another thing entirely to put the idea into practice, he discovered. After all, this was the first time he had asked a woman out since the accident, and it wasn't just any woman but Heather. That made a whole world of difference.

'Where to?'

'Oh…um…a walk in the park, a show, dinner—whatever you fancy.' He saw her open her mouth and knew that she was going to refuse. Despite his qualms he hurried on. 'My flat's a tip at the moment. There's boxes of stuff piled up in every room. If I have to spend the weekend stuck in there, I'll go mad. I need to get out and I just thought you might like to come with me if you don't have anything planned.'

'I see.'

She paused, obviously weighing up the idea, and Archie held his breath. He would understand if she refused. She was bound to have doubts in the circumstances and he wasn't going to try to persuade her to do something that didn't feel right. However, he couldn't deny that he was mentally willing her to accept.

'OK.' She gave a little shrug. 'I would hate to think of you languishing in the midst of all that mess so, yes, I'd like to come. It will make a nice change for me, too,' she added as she stood up. 'I've not really been anywhere since I moved down here and it will be good not to have to stare at the same four walls all weekend.'

'Great.' Archie smiled, hoping she couldn't tell how mixed up he felt. It was hard to decide which took precedence, delight at the thought of them spending time together or trepidation at the idea of getting into a situation he might not be ready to handle. 'How about I pick you up around ten o'clock on Sunday morning and we go from there? There's loads of things to do in London so we'll see what takes our fancy, shall we?'

'We can both be footloose and fancy-free for the day,' she said lightly, and he chuckled as delight surged ahead and took pole position.

'We can.'

She told him her address then left. Archie finished his meal, lingering over a second cup of coffee because he was in no rush to face the traffic. By the time he left the café, the worst of the rush hour was over and it took him less time than usual to drive home. As he pulled into the forecourt of the block of flats where he lived, he felt better than he'd done for a long time. Knowing that he would be seeing Heather on Sunday had given him a boost, although he knew that he mustn't get too carried away.

Come the end of the month he would be leaving London. *That* wasn't going to change.

The weather was very overcast when Heather woke up on Sunday morning, a bank of heavy cloud obliterating the sun. She dressed accordingly, donning jeans and a T-shirt, topped off by a thick sweater. Comfortable boots and a cosy hooded parka in a muted shade of green completed her outfit. Although she had no idea what Archie had planned for them, she intended to be prepared and added a long woollen scarf and a matching pair of gloves. Come hail, rain or shine, she was ready for it!

Archie arrived shortly before ten, tooting his horn as he drew up outside. Heather let herself out and ran up the basement steps. He got out of the car and opened the door for her, smiling as he took stock of her all-weather garb.

'I see you're well prepared,' he teased her, helping her into the passenger seat.

'Too right I am.'

Heather returned his smile, thinking how good he looked that day. Like her, he was wearing jeans with a navy polo shirt and a chunky sweater over the top. The puffy down jacket tossed onto the back seat indicated that she'd been right to assume they would be spending the day outdoors. He looked so ruggedly handsome as he strode around the car that she couldn't help the little frisson that ran through her. Despite her initial qualms about going on this outing, there was no doubt at all that Archie was a very attractive man, and that she was attracted to him.

'Unless you have a better suggestion, I thought we'd start the day at Kew Gardens.' He started the engine of the expensive convertible, revving it to a throaty roar that made her body start to hum as well.

'Sounds good to me,' she agreed, doing her best to keep everything tamped down to a more decorous level. Although she and Ross had had an intimate relationship, she had never found their love-making particularly fulfilling. She had put it down to her own lack of experience and told herself that it would improve with time. Now she found herself wondering if that would have happened. Although Ross was an extremely handsome man, she had never responded to him the way she found herself responding to Archie.

She bit her lip in sudden panic. Everything seemed to be moving far too fast all of a sudden and she was afraid that she would get swept away if she wasn't careful.

'If you're not sure about this, Heather, we don't have to go.' Archie must have sensed her indecision. He reached for her hand and gently squeezed it. 'It's your choice.'

'I do want to go, though,' she said truthfully. She sighed because there was no point lying. 'I just don't think it would be wise for us to get in too deep at the moment, Archie.'

'I understand. Really I do. And I agree with you.' He gave her fingers a final squeeze then released her. 'So what's it to be? A jaunt round Kew Gardens followed by lunch and a visit to one of the art galleries, or a day devoted to washing your smalls?'

She chuckled. 'Some choice! I'd have to be mad to opt for the latter, wouldn't I?'

'You certainly would.' He grinned wickedly as he put the car into gear. 'Although far be it from me to have pointed that out to you. You needed to realise it yourself.'

'Thank you!'

Heather laughed as her doubts disappeared almost as quickly as they had come. She could do this, she really could. She could have fun with Archie, enjoy his company and give thanks for the fact that he was turning out to be such a good friend. She was a grown woman in charge of her own life and she could handle anything that came her way!

* * *

They spent the morning wandering around Kew Gardens and still only managed to see a small fraction of it. Heather was entranced by everything they saw—the Pagoda with its wonderful view over the grounds, the newly restored Kew Palace, the huge glasshouses with their priceless collections of rare plants. Archie was delighted by her reaction and discovered that he enjoyed himself even more because she was having such a good time. By the time they headed back to central London for a late lunch, he was certain the day would do them both the power of good.

He'd booked a table for them at The Ivy, shamelessly playing on his title to secure them a prime position so that Heather could watch all the celebrities who were lunching there. She stared at him after they were seated at their table by the hostess.

'*Sir* Archie? Do you really have a title, Archie?'

'I'm afraid so. I don't use it normally, but it comes in very handy when you want a decent table.' He winked at her. 'I don't fancy sitting next to the kitchen, do you?'

'No.' She chuckled. 'You really are shameless. Exploiting your family connections for your own ends.'

He held up his hands. 'Guilty as charged, your honour.' He laughed when she rolled her eyes. 'Actually, it was a game Duncan and I used to play when we were younger. If anyone from the estate wanted to go somewhere—to a restaurant or to see a show—we'd phone up for them and pretend to be our father. It's amazing how quickly folk respond when you start name-dropping.'

'Shameless and *devious*.' She shook her head. 'I must remember that.'

'I'm only ever devious in a good way,' he assured her, laughing.

He picked up the menu, realising it was the first time in ages that he'd thought about his brother and not got upset. He and Duncan had been very close when they'd been younger so that what had happened had been all the more painful. He'd been both hurt and angry about what he'd seen as Duncan's betrayal, but all he felt now was a deep sadness that they had parted on such bad terms.

They ordered their meal and had a glass of wine while they waited. Archie just sipped from his glass, conscious of the fact that he would have to drive Heather home later. When the meal arrived it was very good—exquisitely cooked, using the very best ingredients. Heather ate with relish and he liked the fact that she didn't pick at her food like so many women did.

'That was delicious,' she declared, setting down her cutlery.

'Better than the food at the café,' he said, arching a brow.

'Not better. As good as,' she said decisively, and he laughed.

'I'm not sure the chef here would be thrilled to hear that.'

'Then I won't tell him if you won't.' She put her finger to her lips. 'It will be our secret, Archie. OK?'

'Fine,' he agreed, his heart pumping away inside his chest as though it was on a mission to escape. He scooped up the last morsel of food off his plate, trying not to think about how much he wanted to press *his* fingers to her lips, but it was impossible to rid himself of the thought of how smooth and soft they would feel, how very tempting. He took a deep breath as the waiter arrived to remove their plates. This was getting out of hand and he had to stop all this fantasising.

The waiter gave them the dessert menu but Archie opted just for coffee. Heather decided that she could manage a dessert and chose a rich chocolate brownie served with whipped cream. She groaned after she'd finished eating it.

'I am stuffed to the gills. I'm not sure if I can

manage to walk round that art gallery. The way I feel at the moment, you might have to carry me.'

Archie smiled. 'I feel a bit that way myself. How about we leave the gallery until another day?'

'If you like.' She glanced at her watch. 'It's almost four anyway, probably time we went home.'

'You can go home if you want to, or you could come back to my place.' He shrugged, wondering if it was wise to suggest it. However, he really couldn't bear the day to end just yet. 'The couch is still *in situ* so there's somewhere for us to sit, and I haven't packed up the stereo yet so we can listen to some music if you like.'

'I'd like to see where you live, Archie, but are you sure it's a good idea?' She leant forward and he could see the doubt in her eyes. 'You're going back to Scotland at the end of the month and I don't know what I'm going to be doing after that. Are you sure it's wise for us to spend any more time together?'

'No, I'm not sure,' he said truthfully. 'It could be a big mistake for all I know, Heather.'

'But you still want to go ahead?'

'Yes. I know it's the wrong time for us to get involved. There's too many other issues going on in our lives. But I can't deny that I enjoy being with you, and I think you feel the same way.'

'I do.'

Her voice was so low that Archie had to strain to hear it over the noise of the other diners. However, it was obvious that she had serious doubts and she was right to have them, too. The last thing Heather needed was him disrupting her life.

'Forget it,' he said quickly. 'It was a stupid idea.'

'No, it wasn't.' She placed her hand on the table, palm up, and smiled at him. 'It's been ages since I've had so much fun. I'm loath to see the day end, too.'

Archie stared at her hand for a moment then slowly placed his hand on top of hers. Her fingers felt so small and so fragile as they closed around his that he was beset by fears once more. He wouldn't be able to live with himself if he ended up hurting her. He had ruined so many lives and he couldn't bear to think that he might ruin Heather's as well.

CHAPTER SEVEN

BY THE time they reached Archie's flat, Heather was starting to wonder if she should have gone home with him after all. It was all very well claiming that she intended to look towards the future, but she couldn't ignore everything she'd learned in the past. Her previous relationship had been a disaster so what guarantee was there that this wouldn't turn out the same way? The thought of losing Archie's precious friendship was more than she could bear.

'I'm not sure if this was such a good idea,' she said as they drew up. 'I don't want to spoil what we have, Archie. I value your friendship far too much.'

'Me, too.' He gave her a crooked smile as he switched off the engine. 'How about we have a cup of coffee now that we're here and then I'll take you home? Would you be happy with that?'

'Yes,' she said slowly. 'That sounds all right to me.'

'Good.'

He got out of the car and led the way to the main doors of the building. Heather knew how expensive property was in this part of the city and couldn't help being impressed when he ushered her inside. A huge, marble-floored foyer opened out from the vestibule with stairs on one side and lifts on the other. There was a reception desk tucked into an alcove, manned by a porter who greeted Archie with a smile.

'Afternoon, Mr Carew.'

'Good afternoon, Pete.' Archie drew her forward and introduced her. 'This is a friend of mine, Miss Thompson. Heather, this is Pete, one the team who look after this place.'

'Nice to meet you, Pete,' Heather replied, shaking the man's hand.

They took the lift up to the third floor and Archie let them into his flat. As he had warned her, there were cardboard boxes and packing cases in every room but not even the clutter could detract from the grandeur of the place. With its high ceilings and wonderful plaster-work, it was a real jewel and Heather sighed as she compared it to her own drab abode.

'This place is gorgeous. It's so light and airy.'

'I know. I've loved every minute of living here, too.' Archie unlocked the French windows that led onto a balcony. 'Come and look at this view. It's stunning even on a miserable day like today.'

Heather followed him out onto the balcony. She could see right across the river from where they were standing, see the yachts moored in the nearby marina. As she watched, a helicopter swooped low and landed on the opposite bank of the river.

'That's the heliport,' Archie told her. 'A lot of people around here use it. It's more convenient than trying to get in and out of the city by car.'

'It's a whole different world. Private helicopters and yachts are way beyond the reach of most people.'

'The rich and their toys,' he teased her, and she laughed.

'Something like that.'

They went back inside. Archie lifted a pile of medical journals off the couch and plumped up the cushions. 'Sorry about the mess. As I explained, I'm trying to get everything sorted before the end of the month. I just never realised how much stuff I'd collected over the years.'

'You've lived here for a while, then?' she asked, sitting down.

'Oh, yes. Ever since I moved to London.' He must have seen her surprise and explained. 'The flat is actually owned by the estate. That's how I was able to afford to live here when I first qualified. I pay only the most minimal rent, definitely not what I'd have to pay on the open market.'

'Lucky you!' she exclaimed, and he grimaced.

'I know. And I do feel guilty about it at times, too.'

'Don't be silly, Archie. It isn't your fault if your family is wealthy.'

'No, I don't suppose it is.' He piled the magazines on top of some boxes. 'How about that coffee? Or maybe you'd prefer a drink. I've got some wine in the fridge if you fancy a glass.'

'Thanks, but I'll stick to coffee so long as it isn't any trouble,' she added, glancing at the surrounding clutter.

Archie laughed. 'Don't worry. The coffee-maker will be the last thing I pack!'

He disappeared into the hall and Heather heard his footsteps crossing the parquet floor as he made his way to the kitchen. She took a deep breath as she settled back against the cushions. So far, so good. Nothing had happened to make her wish that she had gone straight home. She was enjoying herself, as she always did when she was with Archie. If only they'd met at another stage in their lives, she thought wistfully. The outcome could have been very different then.

Archie was glad to have a few minutes to himself as he filled the coffee-maker and set it to drip. Having Heather in his home felt so right that it scared him. He couldn't remember feeling this comfortable with anyone before, not even Stephanie.

He sighed. Stephanie had been the woman he'd been intending to spend his life with and he felt guilty about having such thoughts. However, he couldn't lie to himself. He had to face the facts no matter how painful they were: he had never felt as at ease with Stephanie as he felt when he was with Heather.

He sat down at the kitchen table while he let the idea settle in his mind. Was it true or was it merely a cover for his real feelings? Did he prefer to think that he and Heather shared a special kind of rapport rather than admit that he wanted her sexually?

He tested out that theory but he wasn't convinced it was true. Although he was attracted to Heather, it didn't alter the fact that he felt more in tune with her than anyone else, *including* Stephanie. Stephanie had been beautiful and clever, witty and charming, but there'd always been a certain distance between them. He'd never felt as though they had meshed completely even though he had loved her very much.

Or thought he had.

The thought brought him up short. He had never doubted his feelings for Stephanie before, so why was he doubting them now? Even when he'd found out that she and Duncan had been having an affair, he'd kept on loving her—or so he'd assumed. Now, for the first time ever, he found himself wondering if it had been an overwhelming sense of betrayal that had caused him so much pain. His pride had been wounded, his faith had been shaken, but had his heart been broken?

The coffee-maker gurgled to a stop and he stood up, took two cups out of the cupboard and placed them on a tray along with the carafe. He found the sugar bowl and poured some milk into a jug then carried everything into the sitting room. Heather was sitting on the couch and his heart seemed to swell to double its normal size as he studied the sweetness of her profile. Was this what true love felt like, this overwhelming tenderness he felt whenever he was with her, this desire to protect her from harm and cherish her? He didn't know. He'd thought he'd found love before and lost it, too, but he was no longer sure any more. All he knew was that he felt differently when he was with Heather.

'Mmm, that smells good. Obviously it's not instant.'

Archie jumped when Heather turned and

smiled at him. It was an effort to disguise how on edge he felt as he crossed the room and set down the tray. To suddenly discover that his feelings for Stephanie might not have been as deep as he'd assumed they'd been was scary. In some indefinable way it altered everything that had happened and forced him to reassess the situation. If he'd not been in love with Stephanie then he had no right to feel bitter about her and Duncan.

The idea was far too complex to deal with it right then. Archie drove it from his mind as he picked up the carafe. 'Help yourself to milk and sugar,' he said, handing a cup to Heather.

'Thanks.' She added a splash of milk to her cup then took a sip. 'Excellent. If you fancy another career change, you could earn a fortune running your own coffee-bar.'

'Maybe I'll open one on the estate,' he replied lightly, adding both milk and sugar to his cup.

'Good idea.' She took another sip of her coffee then looked at him. 'Are you sure you're doing the right thing, Archie? It's obvious how much you adore your job and it seems crazy to give it up and do something else.'

'Believe me, I've thought about it a lot and it's the only solution.' He tipped back his head and stared at the ceiling. 'Running the estate is a full-time job and there's no way I can combine it with my work. I'm just not prepared to give my patients anything less than a hundred per cent commitment.'

'I understand that, but why should the estate take precedence?' she protested. 'I know how hard you must have worked to reach your present position. It's a crying shame all that experience you've gained will go to waste.'

'I really don't have a choice. I need to ensure that the estate is run properly, the way my brother intended it to be run.'

'I doubt he would have expected you to sacrifice your career for it.'

'Maybe not,' Archie agreed, stung by the

comment. Duncan would never have expected him to give up medicine to take over the estate. In fact, his brother would have been horrified by the idea. But Duncan wasn't here any more and it was all Archie's fault. That was why he had to do this, to make up for the fact that his actions had resulted in his brother's death.

'But you're determined to go through with it anyway?'

'It's something I have to do, Heather.' Just for a moment he toyed with the idea of telling her the whole sorry story but what was the point of doing that? The last thing he wanted was to burden her with his problems.

'In that case, I only hope you don't regret it, Archie.' She leant forward and he could see the concern in her eyes. 'Promise me that if it doesn't work out, you'll reconsider your decision. I…well, I would hate to think of you being unhappy.'

'I promise.' He placed his cup on the table

and reached for her hand. 'Thank you for caring, Heather. I really appreciate it.'

'I'll always care what happens to you, Archie,' she said softly.

Her eyes rose to his face and his breath caught when he saw the expression they held. It wasn't as bold as an invitation but he knew all the same that she wanted him to kiss her. He drew her towards him until there was only the tiniest gap separating them. This close to her he could see how finely textured her skin was and couldn't resist running the pad of his thumb across her cheek.

'Your skin's like satin,' he murmured, and she shuddered.

He wasn't sure if he moved then or if she did, but all of a sudden there was no longer any gap between them. Archie felt shock sear through him as their mouths met for the very first time. Heather's lips were so deliciously smooth and soft that he groaned. Kissing

Heather was even better than he had imagined it would be!

Their mouths meshed, clung, then reluctantly drew apart. Archie could feel a tremor working its way through his body and knew that Heather could feel it, too. Maybe he should have tried to disguise how he felt, but what was the point? In a couple of weeks' time they would go their separate ways and this would become just a dim and distant memory.

It was painful to realise how short-lived these feelings could be. He brushed his fingers across her mouth and sighed when he felt her tremble this time. 'At least I'm not the only one who feels poleaxed.'

'No.' She gave him a shy smile. 'You're a great kisser, Archie Carew.'

'Ditto, Miss Thompson,' he whispered, going back for a second kiss. Maybe it was madness but he simply couldn't resist the temptation of her lips.

He kissed her long and hungrily this time, but she responded with equal fervour and he was glad about that. He didn't need to worry that he had coerced her when he felt her eagerly returning his kisses. He wasn't sure what would have happened next. He doubted if Heather would have called a halt and knew that he certainly wouldn't have done but the decision was taken from them when the telephone suddenly rang. He sighed as he broke away from her and stood up.

'I'll have to get that in case it's work,' he explained, heading into the hall.

It was Gina Davidson, his junior registrar. Archie listened with mounting concern as the young doctor explained why she was calling. 'You did the right thing by phoning me,' he said, cutting short her apologies. 'I'll be there as soon as I can. In the meantime, tell Wendy that under no circumstances are the parents to be allowed in to see her. Is that clear?'

He hung up after Gina promised to pass on his instructions. Heather looked at him in concern when he went back to the sitting room and he guessed that his expression gave away more than a hint about his feelings.

'Emily Jackson has been admitted with a ruptured spleen,' he said without any preamble. 'According to her parents, she fell off her bike, but A and E didn't believe them. They checked Emily's notes and discovered that I'd had concerns, too, so they asked Gina to phone me. I said I'd go straight in.'

'The poor little thing!' Heather exclaimed, standing up. She followed him out to the hall. 'Did you get any feedback from the social workers?'

'Not yet. Apparently, Emily's father works for the Foreign Office and the family has been living abroad for the past few years.' Archie scooped up his car keys and opened the front door. 'They're still investigating but it's difficult to get information about possible child abuse in a situation like this.'

'I can imagine.'

They went down in the lift and out to the car park, but Heather stopped when he hurried over to his car. 'I'll make my own way home, Archie. It's more important that you see to Emily.'

Archie shook his head. 'I'm not leaving you to trail across the city on your own.'

'I'm a grown woman. I'm perfectly capable of getting on a bus.'

'I'm sure you are but just humour me, eh?' He unlocked the car and opened the door for her. 'I'll feel happier if I know you're home safe and sound.'

She sighed as she slid into the seat. 'Well, I certainly don't want you worrying about me. You have enough on your plate with poor little Emily.'

Archie didn't say anything. It didn't seem appropriate to tell her that he would always worry about her. He drove her home then set off for the hospital, trying not to dwell on the thought that in a few weeks' time Heather would be on her own. As she'd pointed out, she was a grown woman and more than capable of taking care of herself. The problem was that he would love to be able to take care of her if she would only give him the chance. Looking after Heather would be a pleasure, not a chore.

CHAPTER EIGHT

IT WAS Monday evening and once again Heather had arrived early for work, only this time it had been deliberate. She'd not heard from Archie since he had dropped her off at her flat and she was longing to find out what had happened about little Emily. That she was also longing to see him was something she tried not to think about. There was no future for her and Archie, and there was no point getting too attached to him.

She sighed as she made her way to the paediatric unit. It was good advice but it was a tad too late. She was already more involved with Archie than she should have been. Those kisses they'd shared were proof of that. If he hadn't received that phone call, they would have ended up in bed together and that certainly wouldn't have been the right thing to do.

She had never slept around. Whilst many of her friends had thought nothing of having a one-night stand, Heather had never been able to treat sex so casually. There needed to be an emotional bond as well as a physical attraction before she could consider sleeping with a man, and even then there was no guarantee it would work out right if past events were anything to go by.

It was worrying to realise how close she'd come to making a mistake. Even though she had been longing to see Archie when she had set off that night, it was a relief when there was no sign of him on the ward. Heather got straight down to work, helping Abby make up a bed for a ten-year-old boy who had been admitted via A and E. They had just finished when the child arrived and her heart fluttered wildly when she discovered that Archie had accompanied him to the ward.

'This is Adam Regis,' Archie explained as the porters positioned the trolley next to the bed. 'He had a bit of squabble with a bus and ended up with a bump on his head. He has a mild concussion so I've decided to keep him in overnight as a precaution.'

'Hello, Adam,' Heather said, smiling at the boy.

They got him settled then Abby was called to the office to sort out a query about the linen supply. Heather checked Adam's notes and saw that he was down for half-hourly obs. She checked his vital signs and noted them down on the chart, and all the time she was doing so, Archie was watching her. He took the chart from her after she'd finished and read through her notes.

'That looks fine. I just want to make sure that nothing untoward happens in the next few hours.'

'I'll keep a close eye on him, Mr Carew,' she said formally, and he smiled at her.

'I know you will, Heather.'

He turned to speak to Adam then but Heather

could feel herself blushing as she recalled the warmth in his eyes. She groaned under her breath. Being sensible wasn't going to be easy if Archie looked at her like that too often!

'I want you to get some rest now, Adam,' Archie was saying, his attention firmly focused on the child now. 'Your parents should be here shortly and the nurse will bring them in to see you when they arrive.'

He glanced at her for confirmation and Heather nodded. 'Of course.'

'My dad will go ballistic,' Adam muttered, his lower lip wobbling ominously. 'He told me that I wasn't to go out on my bike after school but I wanted to go to the shops so I took no notice of him.'

'I'm sure your dad will be more relieved that you're all right than anything else,' Heather said soothingly.

'You don't know my dad,' Adam replied miserably.

Heather sighed as they left the boy to rest. 'I hope we don't have another aggressive parent to contend with.'

'I'll have a word with Mr and Mrs Regis when they arrive and make it clear that it won't achieve anything to shout at him.'

'Good.' She gave him a quick smile, trying to contain the feeling of excitement that rose inside her when he smiled back. 'What's happened about Emily? I see from the board that she's in the high-dependency unit.'

'That's right. I had to perform a splenectomy so she needed a few days of intensive nursing.' Archie sighed. 'I was hoping to re-implant a small section of healthy tissue in case the spleen would regenerate itself. It does occasionally happen in children but, sadly, Emily's spleen was too badly damaged for that.'

'What a shame. Did you get to the bottom of what had happened?'

'No. The parents insist it was an accident but I

still don't believe them. I've passed the case over to the police and asked them to look into it.'

He glanced round then ushered her into the sluice room when a couple of visitors arrived. Heather guessed that he didn't want anyone to overhear them but she couldn't help feeling even more keyed up when he closed the door and they were alone. She had to force herself to concentrate as he continued.

'Emily's father has threatened to sue me and the hospital if we continue to deny him access, but that's a risk I'm willing to take. There is no way that I'm allowing him to see the child if he's the one who hurt her.'

'Has Emily said anything?'

'No. The poor little mite is terrified, and the mother's exactly the same. She clammed up when I told her that we suspected Emily's injuries weren't accidental.'

'I take it that she's allowed to see Emily?' Heather queried.

'Oh, yes. The poor kid's been through enough without us cutting her off from her mother as well.' He glanced round when he heard footsteps outside the door. 'Anyway, I'd better let you get on. I'll be here for another hour or so. If you need anything, just phone my office.'

'Thank you. I will.'

Heather went back to the ward. It was time for the evening obs so that kept her busy. However, more than once she found her thoughts straying to the conversation they'd had. In truth it had been nothing out of the ordinary—they'd spoken about the usual things that a doctor would discuss with a member of his staff—but it had meant more than that to her.

After a couple of months working as an agency nurse, Heather had grown accustomed to being viewed as just someone who filled in the gaps, but Archie hadn't treated her that way. He never had. It brought it home to her all of a sudden how much she missed the responsibility she'd had at Dalverston General.

As a senior staff nurse on a busy ward, she'd been used to making decisions and acting on them. She knew that she was good at her job and that if she'd stayed in Dalverston, she would have been offered a sister's post this year. However, if she carried on doing agency work, she would never fulfil her true potential.

It made her see that she must find herself a permanent post so she could continue her training. It made sense, too, because the better qualified she was, the easier it would be to find a job anywhere in the world. Maybe she should think about taking a post in Scotland, she mused as she jotted down Adam Regis's obs. That way she could continue to pursue her career. After all, it was mainly thanks to Archie that she had got this far. With his continued support she would soon be back on track.

Heather bit her lip when she realised that it

was just an excuse. It was less her career she was thinking about than seeing Archie. Maybe she was going to miss him, but she needed more time to get over what had happened with Ross, not to mention the fact that Archie had given no indication that he wanted to see her after he left London. He might be happy enough to spend time with her right now, but he certainly wasn't looking for a lifetime's commitment.

Archie remained in his office for over an hour but there were no phone calls. In the end, he was forced to accept that his services weren't needed and left. He sighed as he made his way out to his car. He was acting like an idiot by hanging around in the hope that Heather would call him. Surely he had better things to do with his time?

He drove home, stopping off on the way at the local Chinese restaurant to buy a takeaway supper. Despite the piles of boxes stacked in every nook and cranny, the flat looked depressingly empty when he let himself in. It was no longer his home, just somewhere he came to sleep in between going to work.

He took the food into the kitchen and sat down at the table, not bothering with a plate as he ate it straight from the cartons. He'd ordered his favourite meal—sliced beef with ginger and spring onions plus egg fried rice—but he didn't enjoy it. It was no fun eating on his own. He was merely providing himself with fuel to keep his body functioning.

He cleared away then settled down in the sitting room to read. The book had been top of the bestseller list for weeks but it failed to grab his attention. In the end, he gave up and stared into space, thinking about the future and what it held. The thought of abandoning his work filled him with dread. Even though he loved the estate because it was where he'd been born and brought up, he couldn't imagine devoting his life to it. Was he really doing the right thing, or was guilt clouding his judgement?

It was impossible to decide. He was riven with guilt for causing the accident that had cost Duncan and Stephanie their lives, and desperate to make up for it, but was taking over the running of the estate the best way to do that? Or had Heather been right when she'd told him that he should find someone else to do the job?

Archie sighed because everything seemed to come back to Heather. It was hard to believe that he had known her for such a short time when she had taken over his life to this extent. It was Heather he thought about when he woke up in the morning, and it was Heather who filled his mind when he drifted off to sleep. Were these feelings he had for her real, or were they some sort of rebound effect from losing Stephanie?

He tried to convince himself it was the latter but he didn't really believe it. His feelings for Heather were much deeper than that but he had to control them, had to remember that she wasn't looking for a relationship at the moment. Maybe she had kissed him on Sunday, and enjoyed it, too, but it had meant nothing. When he moved to Scotland, Heather wouldn't be going with him.

By nine o'clock that night most of the children were asleep. There was just Emily awake when Heather did her round. The high-dependency beds were housed in an annexe off the main ward and Emily was the only child in there at the present time. One of the ICU staff had been monitoring her during the day but there was no one to cover that night so Heather had volunteered. She smiled at the little girl as she went in.

'Hello, Emily. How are you feeling? Would you like a drink, sweetheart?'

Emily shook her head. Although, physically, she seemed to be recovering from the operation to remove her spleen, she was extremely subdued. Heather patted her hand, hating to see her looking so unhappy.

'I tell you what. I'll finish my round then I'll read you a story. Would you like that?'

Emily nodded solemnly. She pointed to the book lying on the beside table. 'Will you read me this one?'

'Of course I will.'

Heather checked Emily's obs and noted them on the chart then went back to the ward. Adam Regis was next on her list so she woke him up. Although it seemed cruel to keep waking him up all the time, it was essential that a close check was kept on his condition in case any problems developed. Head injuries were always a cause for concern and they needed to be extra-vigilant.

Emily was wide awake when Heather went back. She sat down on the side of the bed, turning on the light so that Emily could see the pictures while she read to her. 'Once upon a time there was a little puppy called Joe,' she began.

Emily listened intently to every word; she even smiled when they got to the last page and little Joe was reunited with his owner. 'That was a lovely story, wasn't it?' Heather said as she closed the book. 'I can see why it's your favourite.'

She tucked Emily in. 'Now you must try to go to sleep. Your mummy will be here in the morning—that will be nice, won't it?'

Emily didn't say anything. She just closed her eyes and snuggled down under the covers.

Heather made her way down the ward. Adam's light was on and she stopped to see if he wanted anything, frowning when the boy failed to acknowledge her when she spoke to him. Bending down, she quickly checked him over and felt her heart sink when she discovered that one of his pupils was much larger than the other. She knew that the boy needed to be seen immediately by a doctor and hurried to the desk to tell Abby.

'Drat! Mike's off tonight, too—he swopped

shifts with Gina because he was going home for the weekend,' the other nurse told her, picking up the phone. She keyed in a number then put her hand over the mouthpiece. 'I hate dragging Archie in but I don't think Gina can deal with this on her own. He ended up coming in on Sunday as well.'

'Yes, I know,' Heather replied automatically. Her heart sank when Abby looked at her in surprise. 'He mentioned it to me,' she fudged, because it seemed safer than admitting that she'd been with Archie when he had received the call. Although they'd done nothing wrong, she knew how quickly gossip could spread throughout a hospital and didn't want everyone talking about them.

'Oh, I see.' Fortunately, Abby had no time to pursue the matter as Archie answered the phone just then. 'Archie, it's Abby. I'm sorry to do this to you again, but can you come in?'

Heather left the other nurse to explain what

had happened and went back to the boy. His breathing sounded a lot more laboured than it had been a short time before so she unhooked the oxygen mask and popped it on him. She'd only just done that when he started to vomit so she quickly removed the mask and rolled him onto his side so that he wouldn't choke. Abby joined her a few minutes later, looking extremely concerned when she saw how quickly Adam's condition was deteriorating.

'I've phoned Theatre and put them on standby,' she explained as she helped Heather clean up. 'Archie's on his way and he'll probably do a craniotomy. In the meantime, he wants us to send Adam for a CT scan.'

'Shall I phone for a porter?' Heather offered.

'No. It will be quicker if one of us takes him there ourselves.' Abby glanced at her fob watch. 'It won't take Archie very long to get here. He only lives in Chelsea so he doesn't have far to travel.'

Heather forbore to say that she knew exactly

where Archie lived. She nodded when Abby asked her if she would take Adam to the radiology unit while Abby contacted the boy's parents. They wheeled the bed from the ward and Abby helped her manoeuvre it into the lift.

'Ground floor,' Abby told her, pressing the button. 'Someone will meet you there. OK?'

'Fine,' Heather murmured as the doors closed.

It took only seconds to reach the ground floor where she was met by one of the radiographers. They followed the main corridor until they reached the radiology unit where the radiologist was waiting for them.

'I thought it was too quiet tonight,' he joked, helping them transfer Adam into a trolley so he could be wheeled through to the room where the CT scanner was housed.

'Sorry. We didn't intend to spoil your evening,' she replied with a smile.

She glanced round when the door opened and felt her heart leap when she saw Archie. He'd obviously just arrived because he was still wearing his coat. He looked so big and so solid, and so utterly dependable as he came over to them that Heather breathed a sigh of relief. Everything would be fine now that Archie was there.

'How's he doing?' he asked, and she forced her brain into action when she realised the question had been directed at her.

'He started vomiting just after Abby spoke to you. His breathing is very laboured as well.'

'Right. Let's get the scan done and see what's going on. It's probably a haemorrhage but I need to know exactly what I'm dealing with. Adam took quite a knock to the right side of his head when he hit the ground, but there's a possibility that the bleed could be on the opposite side if the brain banged against his skull.' He turned to the radiologist. 'All right if I come and peer over your shoulder, Graham?'

'Be my guest,' the other man replied.

'Thanks.'

Archie whipped off his coat and tossed it over a chair then disappeared into the room that housed the monitoring equipment. Images from the scanner would be relayed to the banks of screens so that he could watch what was happening while the scan was being done.

Heather knew that she wasn't needed any longer and wheeled the bed out of the room. Everywhere was peaceful when she got back to the ward and she was glad about that. She'd had enough excitement for one night and she didn't just mean what had happened with Adam either.

She sighed as she stripped off the sheets and washed the mattress. Even though she knew that she couldn't trust her own feelings at the moment, the more she saw of Archie, the more she grew to like and admire him. He was kind and clever, warm and funny, sexy and good-looking. In short, he was everything she admired in a man but it was far too soon to think about getting involved with him or anyone else.

Barely three months had passed since she'd been planning on marrying Ross and look what a mistake that would have been.

She had known Ross for years, too, yet their marriage wouldn't have worked. It simply proved how poor her judgement was and that she mustn't rush into another situation she would regret. Getting it into her head that Archie was the man she wanted to spend the rest of her life with was just plain crazy.

CHAPTER NINE

THE scan showed that Adam had an extradural haematoma on the right side of his head. An artery had ruptured, causing bleeding into the space between the inner surface of his skull and the external surface of the dura mater, the outer layer of the protective covering over his brain. Archie wasted no time getting Adam to Theatre once his diagnosis was confirmed. Gina Davidson was assisting him.

'I'm going to drill burr holes next,' he explained for Gina's benefit. He had already removed the layers of skin, muscle and membrane from the site of the injury and now he needed to remove a section of the skull. 'Have you seen this done before?'

'Just once when I was a student,' Gina replied, looking decidedly queasy as she watched him drill the first hole. 'I wasn't actually in Theatre at the time, though. I was observing from the gallery.'

Archie could remember how he'd felt when he'd seen the procedure done for the first time close at hand and sympathised. 'I know how brutal it looks but it's the only way to get inside the skull. Don't feel embarrassed if you feel a bit faint. Most of us feel the same until we get used to seeing it done.'

'So I'm not a complete wuss,' Gina said dryly, and he laughed.

'No way!'

He made a series of small holes in the boy's skull roughly in the shape of a circle. Once that was done he used a Gigli's saw to cut between the holes until he had a lid of bone which he then folded back. He nodded when he saw the blood clot that had formed underneath.

'There's the culprit. I'll drain it away and clip the artery. With a bit of luck, that should sort things out.'

It was delicate work and he didn't rush as he cleared away the clot then clipped the artery to stop it bleeding. 'How's he doing?' he asked, glancing at Maggie Parker, who was his anaesthetist that night.

'No problem here,' she assured him, her eyes never leaving the dials.

'Good.'

Once he was sure everything was as it should have been, Archie set about putting everything back together. He replaced the bone and stitched the membranes and muscles back into place. There was just the skin that needed stitching now and he decided to let Gina do it because it would be good practice for her.

'I'll hand over to you now,' he told her, moving aside. She was very petite, barely five feet two in her rubber-soled clogs, and he fetched over the step she used so she could see the table. 'Here's your box, shorty.'

'There are laws against people making remarks like that,' she retorted as she stepped onto the box. 'I'll have you know that I'm not short, I'm vertically challenged.'

'Oops! Sorry.' Archie grinned at her, knowing that she hadn't been offended by his teasing. He always tried to promote good rapport between the members of his team because it helped them work well together. 'I must try to get myself up to speed on the proper PC terms before I insult anyone else.'

Everyone laughed at that before they carried on. Gina did an excellent job of closing and Archie told her that when they left Theatre a short time later.

'That was a first-rate job, Gina. You have a natural talent for surgery so I hope you're going to stick at it.'

'I'm going to give it my best shot,' she said happily.

They parted company then. Archie headed to the men's showers and changed out of his scrubs. He checked his watch, groaning when he discovered that it was already one a.m. There was no chance of him going home just yet, however. He needed to speak to Adam's parents first and explain what had happened. He also wanted to be on hand until Adam had come round from the anaesthetic. Although he wasn't anticipating any problems, there was always a chance that something could go wrong and he preferred to stick around.

He dealt with the parents first, explaining in simple terms what had happened and what he had done. They were naturally upset and worried in case there were after-effects from the surgery. Archie assured them that it was unlikely, although he couldn't give them any guarantees. Head injuries were notoriously tricky and even though the problem had been dealt with promptly, there might be some reper-cussions in the future.

He went to check on Adam next. The boy was in the recovery room and his vital signs were good—his breathing was steady, his pulse and heart rate what Archie would have expected post-surgery. He told the recovery room nurse he would check again in half an hour, but that she was to page him if she was worried and left. It was almost two by then and he was gasping for a drink so he headed to the canteen. There was nobody in there at that hour of the night and he had the place to himself. He dunked a teabag in some boiling water, added milk and sugar, then sat down at a table. He had just taken his first sip when his bleeper started tweeting, and he groaned. Why did it always happen whenever he had a cup in his hands?

He got up and went to the phone, keying in the number for A and E. The duty doctor answered and explained that they had admitted a child with suspected appendicitis. Archie agreed that he would see her and hung up, wondering how they'd known that he was in the hospital at this time of the night—not that it mattered, of course. He was hardly going to quibble about the time when a child's life was on the line.

Adrenaline surged through him as he hurried to the door. This was what he was trained to do and he loved every minute of it. It made him see how hard it was going to be to give it up. Maybe it would be easier if he had someone to share his new life with, he thought wistfully, like Heather, for instance, but there was no chance of that happening. Heather needed to work out her own future and he didn't have any part to play in it.

The day shift clocked on at a quarter to six the following morning. Heather waited while Abby did the handover even though nobody expected her to. As an agency nurse, she was simply expected to work the hours she was paid to do, but she couldn't just rush off in case somebody needed to ask her a question. It was another fifteen minutes before the formalities were completed and Abby sighed as they made their way to the staffroom.

'I am absolutely beat. What a night that was.'

'It was hectic,' Heather agreed, opening her locker.

'You can say that again. Between Adam and that kid with appendicitis, it's a wonder we coped.' Abby slammed her locker door and smiled at her. 'You were a real star, Heather. I know I moan about agency staff, but I don't know what I'd have done if you hadn't been here.'

'Thank you kindly.'

Heather grinned at the other woman, feeling heartened by the compliment. There was often a lot of hostility between the permanent staff and any agency workers so she appreciated

Abby's comments all the more. They left the staffroom together and headed to the lift. There were a lot of staff going off duty and Abby got waylaid by one of her friends. She waved to indicate that Heather shouldn't wait for her when the lift arrived.

Heather got out at the ground floor, hoping her bus would be on time. A couple of mornings it hadn't turned up and she was praying it wouldn't happen again that day as she crossed the foyer. She had almost reached the door when Archie caught up with her and she looked at him in surprise.

'I didn't know you were still here.'

'I ended up doing that appendectomy,' he explained, opening the door for her.

'Thanks.' She stepped outside, shivering as a blast of cold air roared across the car park.

'Grr, it's cold!' Archie exclaimed, turning up the collar of his coat.

'It is. I just hope my bus turns up. I don't fancy

hanging around in this weather,' Heather said without thinking as they set off across the car park.

'Why don't I give you a lift?' Archie offered immediately, and she groaned.

'I wasn't angling for a lift!'

'I know you weren't.' He shrugged when she gave him a sceptical look. 'It never crossed my mind. Honestly.'

'Good. I'd hate you to think I was using you,' she said firmly.

'It wouldn't matter if you were.'

He strode along beside her, his hands pushed deep into the pockets of his coat. The wind had whipped a little colour into his face but she could see the lines that tiredness had etched either side of his mouth and couldn't help feeling concerned. Archie gave far too much of himself to his job. He needed to take better care of himself.

'Well, it should matter. You need to think about yourself a bit more.'

'We're friends, Heather. I can't help it if I worry about you.'

Heather felt a lump come to her throat when she heard the sincerity in his voice. 'Thank you.'

'There's nothing to thank me for.' He gave her a quick smile. 'So will you let me run you home? It will save me worrying about you being stuck here if your bus doesn't turn up.'

She rolled her eyes. 'We're in the centre of London. It's not as though I'll be stranded in the middle of the Arctic!'

'Maybe not, although it feels almost as cold as the Arctic this morning.'

He shuddered as another icy blast tore across the car park and Heather found herself wavering. She had to admit that the thought of standing around in this weather wasn't appealing.

'Well, if you're sure you don't mind…'

'I don't.' Archie grinned as he took her arm and briskly led her over to his car.

Heather sighed when she realised that her capitulation had been a foregone conclusion. 'Do you always get your own way?' she said a tad acerbically as he slid behind the wheel.

'Not always, although I can't deny that it's nice to win occasionally.'

His smile was gentle, making it clear that he didn't see her agreement as a personal victory for him. Archie didn't need to boost his ego by proving he was the winner. He was at ease with himself and she found that an extremely attractive trait. Mind you, there was an awful lot about Archie that she found very appealing.

Heather clamped down on that thought as they left the hospital. She'd already decided that she needed to keep a tight rein on her feelings and she intended to stick to that. The morning rush hour was just getting under way but Archie managed to avoid the worst of the traffic. In no time at all they were drawing up outside her flat.

Heather turned to him. 'Thanks. It takes me twice as long to get home on the bus.'

'I'm glad to help.' He peered at the house. 'Do most of your neighbours go out to work through the day?'

'Thankfully, yes. It's just the traffic that's the bugbear. This street is used as a short cut and the noise never seems to stop.' She opened the car door then hesitated. 'D'you want to come in for a cup of coffee before you head off home?'

'I don't think so. You must be ready for your bed.'

Heather shrugged. 'I doubt I'll sleep until the rush hour is over.'

'In that case, I'd love a cup of coffee. Thank you.'

He got out of the car and followed her down the steps. Heather let them in and hung her coat on the peg by the door. Archie shrugged off his coat and hung it up then followed her into the sitting room. Heather sighed when she saw him looking around because it was a world removed from where he lived.

'It's a bit of a dump but I was lucky to find

anywhere in my price bracket. I had no idea that it cost so much to rent in London.'

'The price of property is extortionate,' he agreed, sitting down on the sofa. He tipped back his head and groaned. 'I don't know how you manage to work permanent nights. I'm absolutely shattered after just one night.'

'Ah, but you worked during the day, too,' she pointed out. She headed to the tiny kitchen which was no more than an alcove off the sitting room. 'I'll make that coffee. It might give you a bit of a boost.'

'The way I feel, I could do with some rocket fuel,' he said drolly, closing his eyes.

'I'll see what I can do.'

Heather chuckled as she set about making the coffee. She decided to make some toast to go with it then loaded everything onto a tray and took it back to the sitting room. Archie opened one eye when she went in and smiled when he spotted the toast.

'You must be a mind-reader. I'm starving.'

'I could make you some eggs,' she offered, but he shook his head.

'No, this is great, thanks.' He sat up and helped himself to a slice of toast. There was honey to go with it and he added a large dollop then took a bite. 'Mmm, that tastes good,' he mumbled with his mouth full. 'Have a taste.'

He offered her the toast and after only the tiniest hesitation Heather took a bite. It was ridiculous to feel so on edge, she told herself sternly. It was just an innocent gesture between friends and there was no reason to see it as a prelude to anything more.

The thought sent a spurt of heat flowing through her. Her eyes rose to Archie's face and her breath caught when she saw the way he was looking at her. When he placed the toast back on the plate and reached for her hand, she started trembling.

'You've got honey on your chin,' he said huskily, drawing her towards him.

Heather gasped when she felt his tongue touch her chin as he licked away the smear of honey. She couldn't believe how erotic it was to have him perform such an intimate act. She was trembling when he drew back, her skin burning where he had touched it with his tongue.

'Maybe this wasn't such a good idea. I didn't intend to make a pass at you, Heather.'

'Didn't you?' she whispered, her heart racing when she saw the desire in his eyes.

'Not consciously.' He smiled wryly as he lifted her hand to his mouth and kissed her palm. 'Although maybe the thought was simmering away inside me.'

'It's the wrong time for us to get involved, Archie.'

'I know. You've just ended a relationship and you need time to get over it. As for me, well, there are any number of reasons why I shouldn't be feeling this way.'

Heather felt her heart lurch. Even though she

knew it was foolish to ask, she couldn't resist. 'And how do you feel, Archie?'

'Excited. Apprehensive. Scared because it feels as though I'm on the verge of something momentous happening, something I know in my heart I should prevent.'

'That's how I feel, too. I keep telling myself that it would be madness to get involved with you, but it doesn't make any difference. I can't understand why it's so difficult to be sensible,' she added plaintively.

'That's the point, though, isn't it? Neither of us *wants* to be sensible.' He turned her hand over and kissed her knuckles. 'We've both taken an emotional battering and we need time out from all the stress. Knowing that nothing can come from our relationship makes it feel safer in a way.'

'You really think that's the explanation?' she said, wondering if it was true.

'It's the only thing that makes any sense to

me.' He looked deep into her eyes. 'I would never do anything to hurt you, Heather. I hope you know that.'

'I do. I feel the same about you.'

'So do you think we can share the next couple of weeks and help each other heal?'

'I think so,' she whispered.

She closed her eyes as Archie leant towards her, not wanting to see any hint of doubt on his face in case it reawakened her fears. They could do this, she told herself as his mouth closed over hers. They could enjoy each other's company and when the time came for them to part, they could do that without any regrets, too. All they needed to remember was that this wasn't a commitment, just temporary solace.

She clung to that thought as she drew Archie's head down so they could deepen the kiss. He kissed her hungrily and with passion, yet beneath that there was tenderness as well. Heather felt her heart overflow as he showed her in the most effective way possible that he really cared about her. This wasn't just sex for Archie—it was so much more.

When he stood up and pulled her to her feet, she didn't hesitate. He led her into the bedroom and sat down on the bed then drew her down to sit beside him while he scattered kisses over her cheeks, her brow, the slope of her nose. When he reached her mouth, Heather tilted her face up to his, kissing him back with just as much passion. This wasn't all one-sided. She wanted him as much as he wanted her.

He gave a low groan as he pressed her back against the pillows and unbuttoned her blouse. All she had on underneath was a lacy bra, a wisp of fabric that concealed very little, and she saw the strong bones in his face tighten as he looked at her.

'You're so beautiful,' he murmured as he drew the tips of his fingers across her breasts.

Heather closed her eyes as a wave of longing

swept through her. The feel of his fingers on her skin was sending ripples of need through every cell in her body, tiny shock waves that seemed to intensify as they gathered momentum. She could feel herself trembling as he continued to caress her, his hands skating so delicately over her skin. When he cupped her breasts in his hands and allowed their weight to settle in his palms, she almost cried out.

He ran the pads of his thumbs over her nipples until they formed hard little buds, eager for his touch. She was still wearing her bra and he didn't remove it before he bent and suckled her. Heather gasped when she felt the warm moistness of his tongue through the fine mesh of the lace. It was incredibly erotic to feel the wet fabric clinging to her skin as Archie drew her nipple into his mouth. Nothing she had experienced before had prepared her for this heady rush of sensations and she gasped.

Archie drew back, cradling her in his arms as

he stroked her hair. 'Shh, it's OK. I won't do anything you don't want me to do.'

Heather shuddered as she buried her face against the solid warmth of his chest. It hadn't been a lack of desire that had caused her to cry out like that—just the opposite. 'It's not that,' she whispered, her voice muffled by his body.

'No?' He set her away from him, and she blushed when she saw the question in his eyes.

'No. I wasn't actually…objecting.'

'Oh. I see.' He smiled as he eased her back against the pillow. 'So you don't mind if I do this?' He lavished attention on her right nipple with his tongue this time then looked at her. Heather shook her head. 'How about this?'

He did the same to her left breast then once again drew back, but Heather was incapable of moving a muscle by then. It was left to Archie to interpret how she felt and he managed to do so without any help from her.

He kissed her hungrily then unfastened her bra

and tossed it on the floor. Her trousers came next and they were soon dispensed with. He turned his attention to his own clothes then, tugging his shirt out of his trousers before it, too, was added to the heap on the floor. Heather bit her lip when he stood up to remove his trousers and she was able to study the powerful lines of his body. He looked so wonderfully, gloriously male that she couldn't help feeling aroused by the sight of him, yet it wasn't just his physical appearance that appealed to her so much. It was Archie himself, the person he was inside, the caring, considerate man she was falling in love with.

Fear rushed through as she was forced to confront the truth. She was falling in love with Archie and there wasn't a thing she could do about it.

CHAPTER TEN

ARCHIE could feel his heart pounding as he lay down on the bed and took Heather in his arms. He knew that he was getting in far deeper than he should be doing, but he couldn't stop himself. She was so beautiful and he wanted her so much that it was impossible to listen to what his head was telling him. All he could hear was his heart, and his heart was telling him to make her his.

Desire exploded inside him like a million fireworks going off as he bent and kissed her. Her lips were soft and warm, slightly swollen from his kisses, and he groaned. It was hard to imagine that anything could be better than this, but there were more delights to come, more pleasure he could give her, too.

He ran his hand down her body, tracing the fullness of her breasts, the narrowness of her waist, the curve of her hips. Her skin was as soft as satin as it flowed beneath his hand, creamy pale and enticingly smooth, and he couldn't get enough of the feel of it. His hand moved on, down her thigh, over her knee, along her calf, and he felt her shudder, shuddered, too. It wasn't just him who was deriving so much pleasure from this but Heather as well, and knowing that heightened his wish to make this the most wonderful experience of her life. Maybe Heather would never love him, but he wanted her to have only happy memories of their time together.

He kissed her again then let his mouth follow the trail his hand had just made, his lips skimming lightly over her breasts, her waist, her hips. He paused when he reached her thigh and kissed the soft inner skin then moved on when he heard her draw in a ragged breath. He didn't intend to rush things; he wanted to take his time, make sure that she enjoyed every second of their love-making.

His mouth skimmed over her knee then skated on to her calf where he scattered kisses at random for the pure pleasure of doing so. Her ankle was so slender that it deserved a special stop for more kisses, and her foot, with its classically arched instep, deserved another. Even her toes were rewarded with special treatment—he kissed each pearly pink nail and revelled in it, too. He hadn't realised before how many places there were on a woman's body that could drive a man wild, but he was finding out now. Each kiss he bestowed on Heather was having an equally potent effect on him, too!

Archie groaned when he felt his body protest at the torture he was putting it through. At this rate, there wouldn't be a successful conclusion to their love-making if he didn't ease off.

Rolling onto his back, he took a couple of deep breaths as he fought for control.

'Archie…what is it? Is something wrong?'

The concern in her voice nearly tipped him over the edge but he gritted his teeth. 'I just need a breather otherwise things might not turn out the way they should,' he explained with massive understatement.

'Oh?' She shot a look at him and blushed. 'Oh!'

'Oh, indeed.' He laughed as he drew her into his arms. 'I'll be fine in a minute—I hope!'

She kissed him on the cheek then snuggled against him. Archie did another bit of teeth gritting when he felt her body press itself against the length of his, but quickly realised it was having very little effect. Every tiny bit of him was clamouring to make love to her and to do it soon. Rolling onto his side, he drew her into the cradle of his hips so that she could feel just how desperately he needed her. He didn't want to rush her but he wasn't sure how much longer he could hold back. Her eyes were heavy with desire when they met his, and he realised with a start that she felt the same as he did.

'Make love to me, Archie,' she whispered, her warm breath clouding on his cheek.

'Are you sure?' he whispered back because he needed to be absolutely certain that she was ready and wouldn't be disappointed.

'Yes, I'm sure.'

She moved against him, pressing her hips against his, and he was lost. He kissed her long and hungrily as he entered her, needing the contact between them to be on every possible level. He couldn't bear it if she didn't enjoy this, couldn't stand to think that he hadn't made her happy.

The doubts filled his head for only a second before they melted away. Archie knew then that he had nothing to fear. Heather couldn't have welcomed him so eagerly, so completely, if she hadn't wanted him so much. When she cried out his name just a moment before the world spun out of his control, he knew that he would remember this moment evermore. It was the moment when he discovered how love really felt.

Heather lay in Archie's arms and listened to the rumble of the traffic outside in the street. They had spent the morning in her bed, making love and sleeping in each other's arms. Although she didn't know how Archie felt, she felt at peace, happy, content. It was the last thing she had expected.

She turned to look at him, smiling when she realised that he was fast asleep. He had been such a gentle and passionate lover. Although he hadn't tried to disguise how much he'd wanted her, he had taken great care to ensure that she'd wanted him just as much. She had reached un-dreamed-of heights in his arms and, no matter what happened in the future, she would always be glad that they'd had this time together. She felt healed and at peace with herself and the world.

'Can I open my eyes now?'

Heather gasped when he opened one eye a crack and peered at her. 'How did you know I was looking at you?'

'Intuition?' he suggested, opening the other eye and smiling at her. He gathered her close and kissed the tip of her nose. 'I thought I'd play dead instead of making you feel all self-conscious.'

'You were lapping up the attention, more likely,' she muttered darkly, not sure if she enjoyed being caught out that way.

'Moi?' He tried to look offended but failed miserably, and she chuckled.

'Yes, you, Mr Carew. Never mind coming the innocent. I know what a tricky customer you are.'

'Do you indeed?' He pulled her against him, smiling lasciviously when she gasped. 'And exactly how tricky am I?'

'Extremely,' she retorted, trying to put a little space between them because the feel of his powerful body pressing against hers was sapping her willpower.

'That's not much of an answer.' He closed the gap, his hips moving seductively against hers. 'On a scale of one to ten, where about do I come for trickiness?'

'Eleven,' she shot back, wishing he would keep still. She took a deep breath as her body responded eagerly to his closeness. She wasn't going to give in to this passion again, no way! She would show him that she had a mind of her own and could hold out for however long it needed...

His hips moved again and she groaned when she felt the hardness of his erection pressing against her. She almost gave up and gave in then. It was just stubbornness that stopped her doing what her body longed for her to do.

'Eleven?' He whistled, his green eyes filled with a mixture of laughter and passion. 'I don't think I've ever scored that high before.'

'We're talking about your deviousness,' she said tartly. 'Nothing else.'

'Of course not. It never crossed my mind that we were discussing anything else,' he replied smoothly, smiling into her eyes.

'Good. Then you won't be disappointed, will you?'

'I shall never be disappointed when I'm with you, Heather.'

His tone was gentle, so gentle that she couldn't find it in her heart to persist with this crazy charade. She cradled his cheek with her hand as she looked into his eyes. 'Neither will I, Archie. What happened this morning was a magical experience for me. I…I never imagined I could feel like that.'

His lids lowered and she heard him draw in a ragged breath. 'Thank you. I can't tell you how good it is to hear you say that because I feel exactly the same.'

Heather's heart overflowed with happiness. She was already moving toward him when he reached for her. They made love again and it was every bit as wonderful as it had been before. She knew that she would never experience the joy and fulfilment she felt right then with anyone else. It was Archie who made their love-making so special, and how she felt about him.

A tiny fear seeped into her heart but she drove it out. She wasn't going to waste what they had by worrying about what she was going to lose so soon. They slept for a short time afterwards then took a shower, the two of them somehow managing to squeeze into the tiny cubicle together. It was almost one p.m. by the time they were both dry and dressed. Archie sighed as he checked his watch.

'I hate to do this but I'm going to have to leave. People will be wondering where I am. I never even phoned Mike to warn him that I wouldn't be in this morning.'

'I understand.' Heather kissed him softly on the mouth then smiled at him. 'Duty calls, etcetera.'

'I can think of better *etceteras* to fill the afternoon,' he growled, pulling her to him and kissing her soundly.

Heather kissed him back then slipped out of his arms. She didn't want to put any pressure on him by making him choose between her and his work. 'If you go now, you can probably catch up with a lot of the things you missed this morning.'

'Practical as well as gorgeous,' he said, smiling at her in a way that made her knees go weak. He picked up his coat and shrugged it on. 'I'll see you tonight, shall I?'

'Yes. I'm due in at six.'

'I'll make a point of being in the ward,' he said, heading for the door. He paused and glanced back. 'No regrets about what happened, Heather?'

'None at all,' she said truthfully. 'It was what we both needed, Archie, wasn't it?'

Something crossed his face, a hint of uncertainty, possibly, before he smiled at her. 'It was.'

He didn't say anything else before he left, tooting his horn as he drove away. Heather waved him off then went back inside. She didn't have any regrets about what they had done and she hoped that Archie didn't have any either. She would hate to ruin the next few weeks by wishing that they'd done things differently, or not done anything at all.

She sighed as she switched on the kettle. If only their relationship didn't have a time limit on it, it would have been perfect, but she had to accept the situation as it was. She and Archie would have to pack as much into their time together as possible. At least that way, when they parted, they would have a lot of wonderful memories to look back on.

Archie went home to change first and finally made it into work just before two o'clock. He had expected there to be questions about where he'd been but nobody said a word so he let things lie and carried on as though nothing had happened. The fact that an awful lot, of mind-blowing magnitude, had gone on that morning was nobody's business but his and Heather's.

His heart surged as an image of Heather lying in his arms sprang to his mind. Making love with Heather had been the most wonderful experience but he had to put what had happened into perspective. This was just a temporary arrangement and he mustn't make the mistake of thinking it could become permanent. So long as he remembered that, he should be able to cope.

He did an early afternoon ward round on his own, wanting to touch base and find out what was happening with the various children. Adam Regis was still in ICU and he made a note to check on him later. Little Kojo Arutee had had his op to repair his hernia and was due to be discharged the following day. Archie checked the boy's notes and confirmed that there was no reason to keep him any longer. Surprisingly, Kojo looked very downhearted when he told him he would be going home in the morning.

'You don't want to stay here, do you, Kojo?' Archie asked, sitting down on the side of the bed. 'You must be missing all your friends.'

'I ain't got no friends,' Kojo muttered.

Archie's brows rose. 'How about at school— you must have some friends there?'

Kojo shook his head. 'Nobody will play with me 'cos the teacher will think they're naughty, too.'

'Ah, I see.' Archie smiled at the little boy. 'There's a really easy answer, Kojo. If you stop being naughty, the teacher will stop telling you off and then the other kids will play with you.'

'I don't know if I can stop being naughty,' Kojo said seriously. He looked at Archie with worried black eyes. 'I try to be good and then something naughty happens.'

'That must be very difficult,' Archie said gravely. 'But you're a big boy now and if you know something naughty is going to happen then you can stop it.'

'How?'

'Just think of something really good that you can do instead and the naughty idea will go away.' Archie stood up. 'Think you can do that?'

Kojo nodded solemnly. 'I'll try.'

'Good boy.'

Archie was smiling as he left the boy's bed. The idea of Kojo being led astray by his naughty thoughts was highly amusing, although maybe he and Kojo had something in common. *His* thoughts about Heather had definitely led him astray.

He sighed as he headed up to ICU to check on Adam Regis. He had lost so many people he'd loved—his father, his brother, Stephanie. But losing Heather was going to be an even bigger wrench, one from which his heart might never recover. Maybe he should try to limit the damage while he could, not get any more deeply involved with her than he already was? he thought desperately. Heather would understand if he explained it to her. She was probably as keen as he was to avoid any problems. They could still be friends, of course, enjoy each other's company, but there'd be no more sex.

Not even a kiss? a small voice whispered tantalisingly in his head and Archie paused while he considered the idea. Maybe it would be all right to kiss her, he conceded. So long as they kept it very-low key.

If a kiss was OK then how about a cuddle? the wretched voice persisted, and he frowned as he considered that option, too. Cuddles shouldn't be a problem either, so long as they kept them to a minimum. In fact, the odd cuddle between friends was perfectly acceptable in modern society.

He smiled in relief as he carried on along the corridor. He would cope perfectly well so long as he stuck to the new guidelines. He and Heather could still enjoy the odd kiss and even a cuddle, but that was it. There must be no extras, nothing to push him beyond his limit, nothing like what had happened that morning…

His mind whooshed back in time and he

groaned. Did he really think he could lay down a set of rules and stick to them? The minute he was near her, he would want more than just a kiss and definitely more than a cuddle. Where Heather was concerned there could be no half-measures. He wanted all of her, not just a tiny bit!

It made him see that the next few weeks were going to be the toughest of his entire life. He'd thought the last twenty-one months had been hard and they had been. He'd been to hell and back, but this was going to be so much worse. To be given a glimpse of heaven and know that it wasn't going to last would be sheer torture.

CHAPTER ELEVEN

THE rest of that week flew past, each day seemingly busier than the one that had gone before. Heather felt as though her life was rushing past at dizzying speed. She and Archie spent as much time as possible together outside work. It wasn't easy when she was working nights and he was working days but they managed it somehow.

He met her from work each morning and drove her home then spent an hour with her. Sixty minutes during which time it felt as though she lived a full year. Being with him was such a rich and wonderful experience that every second counted for double, every minute seemed ten times its proper length. By the end of the week

Heather knew that she was in love with him and it was both scary and exhilarating to feel that way. She knew it was far too soon to feel like that but it didn't seem to matter. What had gone on before had no bearing on what was happening now. She loved Archie and for whatever time they had, she would enjoy loving him too.

The weekend arrived and once again Archie took her out. They drove to Brighton and spent the morning wandering around the town, then bought some food and picnicked on the beach. It was the middle of March and the weather was really too cold to eat outside but they didn't care. Archie had brought a couple of rugs with him and they huddled together out of the wind while they ate pâté and crusty bread, softly oozing cheese and grapes, all washed down with a huge flask of coffee which helped to warm the chill from their bones. Heather couldn't remember enjoying a more perfect day and told him that as they strolled back to the car, hand in hand.

'No wonder I enjoy being with you,' he said, smiling at her. 'You're definitely not high maintenance.'

'Oh, so I'm a cheap date now, am I?' she retorted, pretending to scowl at him. 'Maybe it's time I upped the ante, *Sir* Archie, and demanded champagne and caviar.'

'No problem, if that's what you want.' He turned her to face him, kissing her in full view of everyone who was passing. He didn't appear the least embarrassed when a group of teenagers on skateboards started whistling and catcalling either.

Heather shook her head, feeling decidedly flustered as she came up for air and not just because of the attention they were attracting. Archie's kisses were enough to fluster anyone. 'You pick your places, Archie. I mean, anyone could have seen us.'

'I don't care.' He took her hand again, sliding his fingers between hers as they carried on walking. 'Kissing isn't a crime. I can think of a lot worse things that we could be doing.'

'Ye-e-s,' she agreed hesitantly.

'But?' He turned and looked at her. 'There was a definite "but" tagged on the end of that.'

'But I wouldn't like to cause you any embarrassment.' She sighed when he frowned. 'You have a certain status to maintain, Archie. I'd hate it if anyone from the hospital saw us and started gossiping.'

'I doubt if we'll run into anyone down here,' he pointed out. 'But if it does happen, so what? I'm not ashamed of what we're doing, Heather. Are you?'

She heard the hurt in his voice and hurried to reassure him. 'Of course not! I just don't want to make life difficult for you.'

'You're not.' He raised her hand to his mouth and kissed her cold fingers. 'You've made me feel better than I've done in a very long time.'

'I'm glad,' she said simply, and meant it with all her heart.

They drove back to London and Archie didn't ask her if it was all right as he drove straight to his flat. It was what he wanted and he knew it was what she wanted, too. They made love in the big old-fashioned bed in his room and it was so magical that afterwards Heather cried tears of happiness and regret that one day this would have to end. Maybe Archie felt the same because he was very subdued as he cradled her in his arms.

Heather clung to him, storing up the memory of how it felt to have his arms around her, to hold him close and know that for the time being he was hers. If he had told her then that he didn't want them to part, she would have told him how she felt, too, that she loved him and wanted to spend her life with him. But he didn't say anything and she couldn't break the rules by confessing what was in her heart. It wasn't part of their agreement, plus he might not have believed her after what had happened with Ross. She didn't have a good track record when it came to knowing her own mind and Archie was bound to be wary. Why would he choose to set himself up for a fall if she changed her mind again?

Thoughts tumbled around inside her head until she felt quite dizzy with them. When Archie suggested they should go out for dinner, she refused. She needed to be on her own while she got her thoughts together. The one thing she would never do was hurt Archie. That would be too unbearable for words.

Archie felt as though time was running away with him. Every day he woke up meant he was one day nearer to when he and Heather must part. Although he had known from the outset it was going to happen, it didn't make it any easier to bear. The day they'd spent in Brighton had been particularly difficult. He'd came so close to telling Heather that he didn't want to let her go. It was only the fact that she wasn't ready to hear such a confession that had stopped him. Heather needed to get her life together and he mustn't confuse the issue by declaring his feelings, especially when he wasn't in a position to do so. He couldn't forget that he still needed to make amends for what had happened in the past.

He sought consolation in his work, putting in longer and longer hours at the hospital. When Mike Bridges broke his ankle playing squash it just increased the pressure on him. He had to pick up Mike's work as well as his own, cover all the clinics as well as Theatre. The powers-that-be agreed to hire a replacement for Mike while he was off sick, but it would take time to find someone suitable. In the meantime, Archie had to double his workload.

His own replacement was due to start at the beginning of April. He definitely didn't want to leave the new man with a backlog, so he pushed himself to the limit to get everything done. It meant him cutting down on the amount of time he spent with Heather, which wasn't a bad thing in a way, although he missed her dreadfully. It was a taste of how his life was going to be in the future and that thought weighed heavily on him. A future without Heather wasn't something he relished.

Despite the increased workload, life at the hospital carried on as normal. Adam Regis had been moved back to the ward from ICU. There was no sign of permanent brain damage and Archie was extremely hopeful the boy would make a full recovery.

Emily Jackson was moved out of the high-dependency unit, although the restrictions on who could visit her remained in place. The police were still investigating the case but so far they had come up with no evidence to prove that the child had been abused. It was worrying to think that Emily could be sent home with the problem unresolved so Archie had another word with the social workers. They agreed to place Emily on the 'at risk' register so that was something. The child would be monitored and action would be taken if there were any concerns about her safety.

Friday night rolled around and Archie was still in the ward when Heather arrived for duty. He smiled when she came over to say hello, feeling his heart kick up a storm when he saw the warmth in her eyes. He'd not picked her up from work that morning because he'd had an early clinic and it seemed ages since he'd seen her.

'How are you?' he asked, folding his arms before he gave in to the urge to grab hold of her.

'Very well, thank you, sir,' she replied pertly.

'Oh, it's *sir* now, is it? Obviously, we're being formal tonight.'

'Of course.' She glanced over her shoulder and grimaced when she saw Abby watching them. 'I don't think it's a good idea to arouse everyone's suspicions, do you?'

'Probably not,' he conceded. He straightened

up and sighed. 'That being the case, I'd better let you get on with your work. I was just about to head off home so I don't expect I'll see you again tonight. And much as I would love to spend some time with you over the weekend, I don't think it's possible. I need to get the rest of my packing done.'

'Would you like me to give you a hand?'

'I'd love it!' Archie exclaimed, his spirits immediately lifting at the prospect of seeing her.

They made arrangements for the following afternoon, then he bade her a polite goodbye and left. However, there was a definite spring in his step as he made his way to the lift. He hadn't been looking forward to the weekend, but he was now. Even the most mundane task seemed exciting if he could share it with Heather.

It was ten p.m. and Heather was on her own in the ward. Abby had gone to the canteen for her break with Noreen, the other nurse on duty that night. It had been extremely quiet so far and Heather was hoping it would continue that way. She did her rounds, pleased to see that all the children were fast asleep. Usually at least one was awake, but tonight they had all settled down early for a change.

She added a brief note to that effect on the nightly report sheet then went to the office to fetch the laundry list. Abby had asked her if she would count the sheets as once again there was a discrepancy with the linen and she may as well get it done now. She had just unlocked the filing cabinet when she heard the main doors open and frowned. Abby and Noreen must be back from their breaks already.

Heather found the list and went back into the ward to check if Abby wanted her to count anything else, but there was no sign of her. There was no sign of Noreen either yet she was certain that she'd heard the doors open. She looked around the dimly lit ward, feeling distinctly uneasy. If it hadn't been Abby and Noreen coming in, who had it been?

She did a quick circuit of the room, her stomach sinking when she discovered that Emily's bed was empty. She ran to the bathroom but the little girl wasn't in there either. Had Emily woken up and wandered off? she wondered, hurrying to the phone to raise the alarm. It seemed the most likely explanation, although her heart turned over at the thought of the child wandering around on her own. It was only as she was picking up the receiver that she heard a banging noise coming from the day room and discovered that the fire door was open. Had someone entered the ward and taken Emily away?

Heather didn't waste any more time as she phoned Security and explained what had happened. She had just hung up when the other nurses came back and they were shocked when she told them that Emily was missing. The head of security arrived a few moments later, looking very grim when Heather explained that there were concerns about the possibility that Emily was being abused by her father. He immediately phoned the police.

Heather could feel her anxiety growing as she listened to him talking on the phone. If anything happened to Emily, she would never forgive herself.

Archie was just thinking about going to bed when the phone rang. He groaned as he went out to the hall. The call could only be from the hospital at this hour of the night. Talk about no rest for the wicked!

'Carew.'

'Archie, it's Heather.'

Archie felt his heart give an almighty lurch when he heard the panic in her voice. 'What's happened? Are you all right?'

'Yes. I'm fine. It's Emily. She's missing.'

'Missing?' he repeated. 'How can she be missing?'

'I… We… The police think someone has taken her.'

Her voice was quavering with fear and he knew that he had to calm her down. 'Tell me what happened right from the beginning,' he said gently.

'I checked the children as usual at ten o'clock and they were all fast asleep. It had been a really quiet night so Abby and Noreen had gone for their breaks together and I was on my own. Abby had asked me to check the laundry so I went into the office to fetch the list and while I was in there I heard the ward door open.'

'But you didn't see anyone?'

'No. I didn't look. I know I should have done, but I assumed it was Abby and Noreen coming back.'

'That's understandable,' he said soothingly.

'I should have checked, though.' Her voice

rose. 'I should have gone straight back into the ward and checked who it was!'

'Heather, this isn't your fault. You weren't to know something like this would happen so stop blaming yourself. I'll phone the hospital's manager and let him know what's happened then I'll come straight there. We'll sort this out. I promise. Don't worry.'

'If anything happens to Emily…'

'It won't.'

He hung up then because there wasn't time to reassure her that she wasn't to blame. The most important thing was to find Emily before any harm came to her. He phoned the hospital's manager and explained what had happened then grabbed his car keys and left the flat. He assumed the police would go to the Jacksons' home and check if Emily had been taken there. If she wasn't there, they would organise a search, starting with the hospital and its grounds. If he could come up with a place where Emily's father might be hiding her, it would help.

The thought occupied him on the drive to the hospital. As soon as he turned in through the gates, he could see that a search was already under way. He parked his car and showed one of the policemen his identity badge when he was stopped outside the main doors. It was absolute bedlam when he got to the paediatric unit. Most of the children were awake and there were people milling about all over the place.

Archie gathered together the staff and told them to take the children into the playroom and let them watch a DVD. The ones who were too ill to leave their beds would remain in the ward and he would draft in extra staff from other departments to help look after them. It took some time to get everything organised and he had no chance to speak to Heather. The police had a lot of questions they needed to ask him about Emily's physical condition.

Archie explained that although she had recovered well from the operation, she was extremely vulnerable to infection at the present time. Taking her out on such a bitterly cold night could have serious consequences for her long-term health and the sooner they found her the better. Apparently, the family's car was still parked outside their house so unless the father had hired another vehicle, he must have been on foot and that would have limited the distance he could have gone. The thought that Emily might be somewhere in the vicinity was frustrating.

It was after four when they got their first break. The CCTV tapes showed that Emily's father had entered the building shortly before seven that evening. He'd taken the lift up to the paediatric unit and gone into the visitors' lavatories. He had hidden in there until he'd entered the ward several hours later. There was nothing on the CCTV tapes covering the area around the base of the fire escape to indicate that he had taken Emily into the grounds. It meant that the pair might be still inside the building.

The police immediately organised a full-scale search of the hospital. Archie joined in but by the time the day staff came on duty, Emily was still missing. And every hour that passed increased the danger to the little girl. He was desperately worried about her and worried about Heather, too. He couldn't bear to think that she was going to blame herself if anything bad happened to the child.

Heather's nerves were at breaking point by the time she was relieved from duty. She couldn't help blaming herself even though everyone insisted it wasn't her fault. There was no point going home because she wouldn't be able to sleep so she bought herself a cup of coffee from the vending machine in the foyer and took it outside. There were benches dotted about the grounds so she sat down. The police appeared to think that Emily was still inside the building and she prayed they were right. There was a better chance of finding her here than anywhere else.

She finished her coffee and was about to throw the empty cup into the bin when a movement on the roof caught her attention. She frowned as she stared upwards. There was definitely someone up there, although it didn't look like either a police officer or a member of the security staff. Could it be Emily's father? And was it possible that Emily was with him?

Heather ran back inside. The lifts were all in use so she took the stairs, panting as she raced up six flights to the top floor. There was another set of stairs that led to the roof from there, although the door leading to them was usually locked. It wasn't locked when she tried it now, though. It opened immediately.

Heather hurried up the stairs and stepped out onto the roof. There was a flat expanse, like a wide ledge, that ran all around the building, with a steeply pitched area in the middle. There were chimneys too, towering stacks left over from the hospital's Victorian heyday when coal fires had been used to heat the place. And in the shelter of one of the chimney stacks were Emily and her father.

Heather stopped dead. She knew she should fetch the police but she didn't want to scare the man into doing something stupid when he saw them. The wind was bitterly cold as it tore across the roof and all Emily had on were her pyjamas with a blanket wrapped around her. She knew that she needed to get the child indoors as quickly as possible and was trying to work out how to do it when Emily's father looked round and saw her.

'Hi. I'm Heather,' she said quickly when she saw the panic on his face. She took a step towards him then stopped when he backed away. 'I'm a nurse on Paediatrics and I just want to help you and Emily.'

'We don't need your help,' he snarled, clutching the little girl to him. 'It's people like you who stopped me seeing Emily.'

'I'm sorry,' Heather said quietly. She smiled at the little girl. 'Are you all right, poppet?'

Emily nodded. Her little face was pinched with cold and she was shivering violently. 'Daddy's going to take me some place where Mummy can't hurt me any more,' she whispered.

'Nobody should be allowed to hurt you, Emily,' Heather replied, feeling stricken by guilt. It appeared they had completely misread the situation. It hadn't been Emily's father who had been harming her but her mother.

'That's right,' the father said roughly. 'Nobody is going to hurt my Emily ever again. I'll make sure of that, I swear.'

Heather's breath caught as he backed towards the edge of the roof. All of a sudden she knew what he intended to do. He was going to jump off the roof and take Emily with him. She ran forward and grabbed hold of the child's arm. They were just an inch away from the edge and she didn't dare look down.

'Please, don't do this,' she begged him. 'I know it must feel as though you have no choice but this isn't the way. Whatever has happened, it can be fixed.'

The man laughed bitterly. 'Like the way you fixed it by stopping me seeing Emily?'

'We made a mistake,' Heather pleaded. 'But that doesn't mean we can't make things right now that we know the truth. You love Emily and I know that all you want is for her to be safe and happy.'

'Yes, and look what a mess I've made of it.' Tears streamed down his face as he looked at the little girl. 'I didn't keep her safe because I was a coward. I couldn't bear to admit that my wife was making both our lives a living hell.'

Heather felt fear engulf her when she heard the desperation in his voice. It was obvious that he had reached the end of his tether and she had no idea what to say to him. She took a quick breath, praying that she wouldn't make the situation worse.

'It must have been terrible for you both, but you can still make things right. Emily loves you. She needs you to be strong for her now more than ever.'

She held her breath, hoping that she had got through to him. She heard a shout from below and realised that they'd been seen but she didn't dare take her eyes off him. All it would take was one small step and that would be the end for all of them. An image of Archie's face suddenly filled her mind and she was consumed by sadness at the thought that she might never get the chance to tell him how much she loved him.

CHAPTER TWELVE

ARCHIE thought his heart was going to explode with terror as he looked up at the roof. Although the three figures clustered on the edge appeared no bigger than matchsticks from where he was standing, he recognised Heather immediately. He turned and raced back inside the building, taking the stairs two at a time as he made for the top floor. The police were already there and he shook his head when the senior officer ordered him to stay back.

'Emily knows me. She will be far less frightened if she sees me rather than one of your officers. If she gets upset, it will only precipitate matters, and that's the last thing we want. Let me try and talk to her father first.'

The officer obviously saw the sense of that and let him through. Archie stepped out onto the roof, taking care not to startle the other occupants. He could see that Heather had hold of Emily's arm and knew what a precarious position she was in if the father jumped. The thought that she might be dragged to her death was more than he could bear but he had to put it out of his mind if he was to help her.

'Stay back!'

Archie held up his hands when Emily's father ordered him to stay away. 'I'm not going to come any closer until you say I can. I just want to help you, that's all.'

'Like the way you helped me by stopping me seeing Emily,' the man said harshly. 'It's her mother who's been hurting her, not me. You got it wrong, didn't you?'

Archie didn't know what to think. Was it

true? Was Mrs Jackson responsible for Emily's injuries?

'He's telling you the truth.' Heather's voice was low but that didn't disguise the strain it held. Archie's hands clenched when he saw how pale she looked. 'Emily told me that it was her mummy who had hurt her, not her daddy. Isn't that right, darling?'

Emily nodded, although she didn't speak. She seemed unaware of the danger she was in and Archie was grateful for that at least. He took a quick breath as he rapidly reassessed the situation in light of what he had learned.

'Then all I can do is apologise from the bottom of my heart for getting it wrong.'

'And you really think an apology will make up for what you've put me and Emily through these past few weeks?' the man said scornfully.

'No, I don't. It isn't nearly enough but it's a start and we can build on it from here. If you'll bring Emily back inside I promise you that I will do everything in my power to make this situation right.'

'And you think the police will let you do that? I'll probably go to prison for this and there is no way that I'm leaving Emily on her own. I know what her mother's like. She'll convince the police that I'm the guilty party!'

'No. I won't let that happen. I'll make sure the police know the truth. I swear.'

'That's what you say now but it's always the father who gets blamed in cases like this, never the mother.'

The man took a step back and Archie's heart almost seized up with fright. All it needed was another couple of inches and that would be it. He didn't dare look at Heather in case fear overwhelmed him to such an extent that he was unable to function.

'It isn't going to happen in this case. I'll make sure that Emily tells everyone what has really been going on.'

He took a step towards them, stopping imme-diately when he saw Mr Jackson tense. There were just a couple of feet separating them now but even so he couldn't be sure that he would be able to prevent the man from jumping if it came to it.

'I know you think this is the only way out, but it isn't,' he said urgently. 'Maybe you feel guilty because you didn't stop what was happening, but don't let it affect your judgement. We all do things we regret, but it's how we deal with them afterwards that makes all the difference. You can make things right by telling the police the truth. Emily needs you to be strong for her now more than ever.'

The man didn't say a word as he stared down at his daughter. Archie held his breath, hoping that he had got through to him. When Mr Jackson suddenly crumpled into a heap and started sobbing, Archie could have wept as well, only he needed to make sure that Emily and Heather were safe first.

He swept the little girl into his arms then took hold of Heather by the arm and hurried her inside the building. The police had rushed out onto the roof to get Emily's father but he didn't stop to watch what was happening. He shook his head when an officer tried to take the child from him.

'No. She's been through quite enough. I need to get her back to the ward and check her over.'

Nobody tried to stop him again as they made their way to the lift. It arrived almost immediately and they stepped inside. Archie turned to Heather as the doors closed. 'I was so scared when I saw you up there,' he said brokenly, wishing he could hug her to him.

'So was I,' she whispered.

Archie bent forward and kissed her softly on the lips then had to step back when the lift arrived at their floor. Marion Yates was on duty and she soon had everything organised. While she got Emily settled in bed, Archie had a word with the senior police officer and told him everything that

Mr Jackson had said. Heather backed him up, explaining what Emily had told her about her mother being the one who had hurt her.

Once he was sure the police had the facts straight, Archie went back to the ward and examined Emily. She was cold and very upset but it didn't appear that she had suffered any real harm, although they would need to keep a close watch on her for the next few days. He wrote her up for a mild sedative and left instructions that Mrs Jackson was to be kept away from her. He then had to liaise with the duty social worker. Emily would be taken into care while the police investigated the allegations against her mother, but, hopefully, her father would be given sole custody of his daughter eventually.

By the time everything was arranged it was after nine and he was reeling from tiredness and guessed that Heather must be feeling exactly the same. She was in the staffroom when he tracked her down and she smiled as he went in.

'Everything sorted out now?'

'Just about.' He groaned. 'I'm shattered. I'm so tired, in fact, I could prop myself against this door and go to sleep standing up!'

'Me, too. We make a fine pair, don't we?'

Archie hauled her to her feet and kissed the tip of her nose. 'We do indeed. What we need is a nice soft bed and eight hours of uninterrupted sleep.'

'Sounds blissful to me,' she said as she nestled against him.

'Then what are we waiting for?' Archie shooed her out of the door and along the corridor. There was a taxi dropping off a fare outside the hospital and he flagged it down. 'I don't think I'm in a fit state to drive after all the excitement,' he explained, helping her into the back of the cab. 'I'll leave my car here.'

'Another good idea,' she murmured, resting her head on his shoulder.

'Oh, I'm full of good ideas. Especially for after we've had that lovely long sleep.'

'Something to look forward to,' Heather mumbled, closing her eyes.

Archie put his arm around her and listened to the steady sound of her breathing as they drove through the busy London streets. The terror he'd felt that morning was receding but he would never forget what had happened. He'd come so close to losing her and it had made him see how much he loved her. If only he'd been sure that he was doing the right thing, he would have declared his feelings right there and then, but there were so many other factors to take account of. He couldn't bear it if his love became a burden for her.

Heather slept like a log. It was late afternoon when she woke and for a moment she couldn't think where she was before it all came rushing back—she was in Archie's flat, and in Archie's bed, even if Archie himself happened to be absent at that moment.

She smiled as she rolled over onto her side. She could hear water running and guessed that he was taking a shower. It was funny how normal it felt to wake up in Archie's home. She had never felt this comfortable when she'd spent the night at Ross's. She'd always felt on edge the following morning, a little self-conscious, but it was different with Archie. She felt perfectly at home as she lay there in his bed and waited for him to return.

'Aha! Sleeping Beauty is awake, I see. That's a shame. I was hoping I'd get the chance to try the traditional approach of waking you up.'

Heather felt her breath catch when Archie suddenly appeared. He had wrapped a towel around his hips as a concession to modesty but that was all he had on. The rest of him was naked. Her heart began to race as he walked towards the bed. His torso was beaded with moisture, the tiny droplets catching the light from the window so that his skin seemed to glimmer with a golden sheen. More droplets glistened in the heavy down that covered his well-shaped legs. With his dark hair clinging damply to his skull and his jaw darkened by a night's growth of beard, he looked more like a pirate of old than a sophisticated modern-day man, and she couldn't help responding to the sight of him.

'The traditional approach,' she repeated, struggling to contain the desire that was coursing through her veins.

'Mmm.' He sat down on the edge of the mattress and smiled at her. 'You must have read the story of Sleeping Beauty when you were a little girl?'

'I'm sure I did, but it was a long time ago,' she whispered.

'Then I'd better refresh your memory.' He ran a finger down her cheek, pausing when he came to the corner of her mouth, and she shivered in anticipation.

JENNIFER TAYLOR

233

'Sleeping Beauty was destined to remain in slumber until a prince came along and woke her with a kiss. I always thought that was a brilliant idea, didn't you?'

'It depends what the prince was like,' Heather murmured.

'You could be right.' His finger moved a fraction more, just touching the dimple at the corner of her lips before it stopped again. 'So what's your idea of the perfect prince? Should he be dark or fair, tall or short, or what?'

'I'm not sure.' Heather pretended to consider the question, aware that every second they played this game simply heightened their anticipation as to the outcome. 'I don't think I have an ideal hero in mind, to be honest. Obviously, I'd prefer it if he wasn't too ugly, and it would be good if he had all his own teeth, but I'm not too choosy apart from that.'

'I see. So that means I could apply for the role? I mean, I have all my own teeth and people don't usually faint in the street at the sight of me.'

'I don't see why not.'

'In that case, let's give it a go. You close your eyes and pretend to be asleep, and I'll be the prince who wakes you up.' He grinned at her, his green eyes filled with laughter and desire, a truly potent combination. 'I think I should warn you, though, that it might take me a couple of tries before I get it right.'

Heather laughed as she closed her eyes. She was still smiling when Archie kissed her but that didn't matter a jot. Love and laughter went hand in hand when they were together, she had discovered. He was as good as his word, too. He kissed her several times and each kiss was even more glorious than the one before. By the time he raised his head, she was clinging to him.

'I think you make the perfect prince.'

'Thank you, kindly, my lady.'

He rewarded her with another lingering kiss.

Heather kissed him back, feeling closer to him at that moment than she'd ever felt to anyone else. He was her soul mate, the other half that made her whole. They made love with an intensity and passion that stunned them both. Heather knew that she had been given something so precious, so rare, that she would never find it again if she let it go. And it was that thought which made her do what she'd been afraid to do up till now.

She looked deep into Archie's eyes so there could be no mistake. 'I love you, Archie. I know it's too soon to tell you that but I really do.'

He closed his eyes and she felt the shudder that passed through him. When he drew her to him, she clung to him. He hadn't told her that he loved her, too, but sometimes words weren't necessary. She knew how he felt, could feel it in every cell of her body. Archie did love her, too, and it was more than she could have dared hope for, far more than she had expected.

Archie could feel the shock waves rippling around his body as he held Heather against his heart. She loved him—could it be true? He longed to believe it yet he was afraid that she might have misinterpreted her feelings. She had been through a tough time recently and it was easy to understand how she might have made a mistake. He'd been there when she'd needed someone to talk to, someone to help her heal, but it didn't mean that she truly loved him. He couldn't bear to think that in a few months' time she would realise he wasn't the man she wanted to spend her life with. He had been through that experience once before and he couldn't go through it all over again.

He gently set her away from him, his heart aching when he saw the question in her eyes. He wanted to tell her that he loved her, but it would be wrong to put that kind of pressure on her. If, or rather *when*, she realised that she'd made a mistake, he didn't want her feeling guilty about it.

'I'm sure you believe it's true, Heather, but think about it. It's only a few months since you were planning on getting married.'

'I know and, believe me, I've tried not to let it happen. But I know how I feel, Archie. Really I do.'

'Do you? Are you sure it's love you feel and not just gratitude because I happened to be around when you needed someone to talk to?'

She shrank back as though he had struck her. 'Is that what you think, that I can't tell the difference between the two?'

'I don't know.' He shrugged. He hated to hurt her this way. It was only the thought of how much worse it would be for both of them if he accepted her claim. 'I think it's very easy to confuse the two emotions at the moment. There's no doubt that we get on extremely well together, Heather, but are you *sure* it's love?'

'Obviously not where you're concerned, it isn't.' She tossed back the bedclothes and stood up. 'I apologise if I've embarrassed you, Archie. That was the last thing I intended to do.'

'You haven't embarrassed me,' he protested, but he could tell she wasn't listening to him.

He watched in silence as she scooped up her clothes and took them into the bathroom. He knew that he'd made a mess of things but what else could he have done? Accepted that she was in love with him, admitted that he was in love with her as well, then carried her off on his charger so they could live happily ever after? It was only in fairy stories that things like that happened!

Heather turned on the shower then stood numbly staring at the water as it gushed into the tray. Archie didn't believe that she was in love with him and the reason why he didn't believe it was because he wasn't in love with her. If he'd felt even a fraction of what she felt then he would have known in his heart that she was telling him the truth.

A sob rose to her throat but she forced it down. She wouldn't cry or make a scene. The only thing she had left to her now was her dignity and she needed it to help her through the next few minutes. She showered then dried herself off and dressed. There was no sign of Archie when she went back into the bedroom and she was glad about that. Having to talk to him here in this room where all her dreams had been shattered would have been too painful.

She found him in the sitting room, sitting on the sofa, staring at the ceiling. There were deep lines etched on his face which told their own tale about how he was feeling, but she couldn't afford to weaken. 'I think it's best if I went home now. I'm sorry if I embarrassed you. I never intended to.'

He rose to his feet, his green eyes filled with pain as he turned to her. 'And I never meant to hurt you, Heather. That's the last thing I wanted to happen, too.'

'I know.' She gave him a quick smile then hurried to the door, terrified that the fragile grip she had on her emotions might not last if she lingered. To know that she was responsible for the anguish in his eyes was more than she could bear.

'I'll drive you home.' Archie grabbed his keys off the table and followed her, but Heather held up her hand.

'No. I'll get a taxi.'

'There is no way that I'm letting you go home on your own when you're upset,' he said harshly, reaching around her to open the front door.

Heather felt a rush of tears fill her eyes. 'Please, don't make this any more difficult than it already is.'

'I'm sorry. I don't mean to.' He gave a low groan as he pulled her into his arms. 'I've made such a mess of things. I never meant this to happen, Heather.'

'I know,' she said softly, then pushed him away because she couldn't bear to have his arms around her now. Archie had made it clear that he didn't love her and there was no point fooling herself into thinking that he did.

'Don't blame yourself, Archie. You've done nothing except try to help me and I shall always be grateful to you for that.'

'I helped you because I wanted to, Heather,' he said gruffly.

'Which just goes to show what a kind and decent person you are.'

'Am I indeed?' He laughed harshly, his voice filled with pain. 'That's where you're wrong. I'm not some sort of hero. I'm a guy who makes mistakes that other people end up paying for.'

'What do you mean?' she said, her heart lurching when she saw the tortured expression on his face. 'What kind of mistakes have you ever made, Archie?'

'The worst kind.' He leant back against the wall and closed his eyes. 'I told you that my brother had died in an accident. What I didn't tell you was that it was my fault.'

He opened his eyes and looked at her. 'I killed Duncan. I also killed my fiancée. Was that the act of a kind and decent man?'

CHAPTER THIRTEEN

ARCHIE barely registered Heather's gasp of shock. He had reached the point of emotional overload by then, his devastation about the pain he had caused Heather combining with the anguish he had lived with for all these months. He swung round and went back to the sitting room, staring around him with pain-dulled eyes. How many more lives was he going to ruin by his actions?

'Sit down.'

Heather's voice was so gentle as she urged him towards the sofa that he felt a lump come to his throat. He didn't deserve to be treated with such compassion after what he had done.

He sank down on the sofa as the memories flowed through his mind. If only he and Duncan hadn't argued, if only he'd gone after him and tried to stop him, if only…

'Tell me what happened, Archie. To Duncan and y-your fiancée.'

Heather's voice caught on the last word and it was another reason to berate himself. He turned to her, hating himself even more when he saw how pale she looked, how shocked.

'They were both killed in a car crash,' he said simply.

'Were you driving at the time? You said it was your fault…' She trailed off and he sighed.

'No. I wasn't in the car. Duncan was driving. The police said that he overtook a lorry on a bend and then had to swerve to avoid an oncoming vehicle. His car hit a wall and he and Stephanie were both killed. There was nothing anyone could do for them.'

'Then I don't understand how it could have been your fault.'

'Because Duncan and I had had a furious row and that's why he took such a risk. He was always such a careful driver, but he was upset and angry, and that's why the accident happened.' He dropped his head into his hands. He had pictured the scene so many times that it was almost as though he had been there and seen it happen.

'What had you been quarrelling about? It must have been something important if it caused your brother to act so out of character.'

'Stephanie. We argued about Stephanie.'

'I don't understand. Did Duncan not like her?'

'Oh, no. Just the opposite.' He laughed bitterly. 'Duncan and Stephanie drove down to London to tell me that they were in love. They were extremely apologetic, although I don't know why. I mean, they couldn't help it if they'd fallen for each other, could they?'

'And you had no idea?' Heather said slowly.

'No. I was so wrapped up in my work that I

never noticed what was happening.' He shrugged. 'It probably wouldn't have mattered if I had. I don't think it's possible to stop two people falling in love, and even I have to admit that they were perfect for each other. It's just a shame I didn't realise it when they came to see me. If I'd done so they might not be dead.'

'You can't blame yourself! You were bound to be angry when you found out what had been going on.'

'Maybe. But I didn't need to tell them that I never wanted to see them again, did I?' He stood up, too agitated to sit there while the memories that had haunted him filled his head once more. 'The last thing I said to Duncan was that he could go to hell and he could take Stephanie with him. I got my wish, didn't I?'

'Stop it!' Heather jumped to her feet. 'People say all sorts of things when they're angry. You didn't will your brother to crash his car. It was an accident.'

'Which wouldn't have happened if Duncan hadn't been upset.' He shook his head. 'There's no getting away from that fact, Heather.'

'Maybe not, but the accident happened because your brother drove when he wasn't in the right frame of mind to do so. That was his decision, not yours. It was his decision as well to overtake on that bend.'

She put her hand on his arm, hating to see him torturing himself this way. Pain lanced through her as she realised how terrible it must have been for him, having to deal with his grief as well as all this guilt. Not only had he lost his brother and the woman he'd loved, but he blamed himself for their deaths.

'It wasn't your fault, Archie,' she repeated urgently. 'None of it was your fault.'

'I wish I could believe that.'

'You have to try otherwise it will tear you apart. Promise me that you'll think about what I've said.'

'I shall.'

Heather let her hand fall to her side. She wasn't sure what else she could say to comfort him. Some hurts went too deep for mere words and this was one of them. Her heart contracted when she thought about how much he had lost that day. Losing his brother would have been a big enough blow but to lose his fiancée as well in such tragic circumstances would be more than anyone could cope with. Obviously, Archie had loved her very much. He was probably still in love with her, and the thought was like pushing a knife into an open wound. To know that Achie had loved the other woman and would never love her was too much to bear.

'I'd better go. I'll get a taxi outside—there's bound to be one passing,' she said quickly. 'Take care of yourself, Archie, won't you?'

'And you.'

He didn't offer to drive her home this time. Maybe he realised it was best if they made a clean break. Heather let herself out of the flat and took the lift to the ground floor. The porter opened the door for her and offered to get her a taxi when he discovered that she didn't have any transport but she refused. She would make her own way home without any assistance. It really was time that she stopped relying on other people. They had their own problems, some far bigger than hers.

Tears filled her eyes as she made her way along the road. The thought of how Archie must have suffered was too painful. He might not believe that he was a decent man but he was wrong. Nothing he had told her had changed her opinion of him. Nothing ever would. He was the man she loved, even though he could never love her in return.

Archie found to his surprise that he felt much better after he had told Heather about the accident. It was as though by talking about it he had helped to dispel some of the guilt he'd felt.

Several times during that weekend he found himself wondering if he'd been wrong to blame himself when it had been Duncan's actions that had led directly to the tragedy. Maybe it was time to accept that and move on.

Although he seemed to be on the way to resolving that problem, he was very aware that the situation between him and Heather was extremely difficult. He knew that he had hurt her by refuting her claim that she loved him, but he was sure it had been the right thing to do. Nevertheless, it meant that he would have to be extra-careful when he was around her. It wouldn't take very much to reveal his true feelings and he couldn't afford to let that happen.

He resolved to make life as easy as possible for them during their last days of working together. A replacement had been found for Mike and he seemed more than capable of doing the job. It meant that Archie could cut down the amount of hours he'd been working.

There would be no more working late each evening and that meant he could avoid seeing Heather altogether. It would be a huge wrench, of course, but it was essential that he keep his distance.

The plan was fine in theory but it didn't work out in practice. He was just about to leave on Monday evening when he was called to A and E to see a five-year-old girl who'd been bitten by a neighbour's dog. Although her injuries weren't life-threatening, there was extensive tissue damage to her calf, plus some minor damage to her hand. A and E was bursting at the seams so Archie agreed to transfer her to the paediatric unit until the plastics consultant could assess her injuries.

His heart was beating up a storm as he accompanied the little girl and her mother to the ward. It was gone six and Heather would be on duty. He held the door open while the porter steered the trolley through, doing his best to tamp everything down to a more normal level. At this rate, he would have a heart attack when he saw her!

'Bed six,' Marion informed him briskly. She beckoned over a young woman who was hovering beside the kitchen door. 'Ruth, can you help me with this patient, please?'

Archie didn't say anything as they transferred the little girl to the bed, although he couldn't help wondering what was going on. As soon as they had finished, he drew Marion aside. 'What's happened to Heather? I thought she was due to work here until the end of the month.'

'So did I.' Marion sighed. 'According to the agency, Heather phoned in sick today, although I'd take that with a pinch of salt if I were you.'

'What do you mean?' Archie demanded.

'I think it was just an excuse because Heather had had enough. I don't blame her after what happened on Friday.'

'What happened on Friday,' he repeated blankly.

'Emily and the abduction—remember?'

Marion chuckled. 'You're in a worse state than me if you've forgotten about it so soon!'

'Oh, right. Of course.'

Archie covered his lapse as best he could. He told Marion the plastics consultant was on his way and left. Normally, he would have waited for his colleague to arrive but he couldn't bear to hang around. He went straight home and spent the night worrying about Heather. What if she really was sick and stuck in the flat on her own? Maybe he should go round there and check if she needed anything? On the other hand, if it had been an excuse, she probably wouldn't want to see him.

Thoughts tumbled around inside his head but there was no easy solution to the problem. In the end, he realised that he had to accept her decision, whatever the reason was behind it. The simple truth was she was better off without him.

* * *

It was the worst weekend of Heather's entire life. The pain of learning that Archie didn't love her would have been hard enough to bear, but to discover that he was in love with someone else made it doubly difficult. She knew there was no hope of her competing with his late fiancée for his affections. Apart from the fact that he was still traumatised by her tragic death, he must be wary of entrusting his heart to anyone else. He had been hurt on so many levels that she would never be able to help him heal.

By the time Monday came around, Heather knew that she couldn't face seeing him. She phoned the agency and made her excuses, promising that she would get in touch again once she was feeling better. Obviously, it posed a problem, financially. If she wasn't working, she wasn't earning, but that was the least of her worries. Getting her life back together must be her number one concern—if it was possible to do that.

She spent the week wandering around

London, visiting all the tourist sights to fill in the time. It was better being in the midst of a crowd than on her own with only her thoughts for company. Friday arrived, Archie's last day at the hospital. She knew there was a leaving party planned for him because she'd been invited, but she wouldn't go. She couldn't wave him on his way with the requisite smile when he would be taking her heart with him.

In the end she couldn't stand it any longer. She packed an overnight bag and caught the train to Dalverston. Her father was delighted to see her, although she could tell that he was wondering what had prompted her visit. He didn't try to question her, though. He just welcomed her home and she was grateful for that.

Saturday dawned, bright and clear. Heather got up early and made breakfast for them. Her father had a clinic that morning so it meant she was left to her own devices. She decided to go for a walk along the river bank and set off as soon as her father left the house. It was wonderfully peaceful by the water. She walked as far as the weir and was just about to head back home when she saw Ross coming towards her. It was the first time she'd seen him since she had cancelled the wedding and she couldn't help feeling a little awkward as she greeted him.

'Hello, Ross. You're out early as well, I see.'

'It's too nice a day to lie in bed,' he said, smiling at her. Tall and dark with classically handsome good looks, he had set more than one female heart racing since he'd joined the practice. However, Heather found herself unmoved as she looked at him now. He wasn't Archie, not the man she loved.

'Your dad phoned me last night and told me you were back,' Ross said, falling into step beside her.

'Did he?' Heather flushed. 'He shouldn't have done that.'

'He was only trying to help. Don't be cross

with him.' He treated her to a searching look. 'What's wrong, Heather? And before you deny it, I can tell that something's happened. You haven't had second thoughts…?'

'About not marrying you? No. I still believe it would have been wrong to go ahead with the wedding.'

'So do I.'

'You do?' She stopped and stared at him in surprise.

'Yes. After you left it didn't take me long to realise we would have both regretted it if we'd gone ahead. You did the right thing calling it off.' He shrugged. 'So if it isn't that, what is it?'

All of a sudden Heather knew that she had to tell someone about Archie and who better than Ross? He had always been such a good friend to her. That had been part of the problem, in fact—she'd loved him as a friend, not as a lover.

She told him everything: about meeting Archie outside the church and her shock on seeing him again in London; how they had spent time together; the accident that had resulted in the death of his brother and his fiancée. Ross listened without interrupting until she came to the end of her story then sighed softly.

'It's a real mess. No wonder you felt that you had to get away. But are you absolutely sure that Archie doesn't love you?'

'Yes, of course I am.' She smiled thinly. 'He told me that I was confusing gratitude with love, that it was too soon for me to know how I felt. He did his best to put me off, in fact.'

'But did he come right out and say that he didn't love you, Heather?' Ross persisted, and she frowned.

'No-o-o. I don't think so. Why? Does it make a difference?'

'I think it does. I think it's possible the guy is in love with you but he's afraid to reveal his feelings in case you've made a mistake about yours.' He held up his hand when she opened her mouth to protest. 'I'm not saying you have. I just think it's what he believes. You can't blame him for being wary after what he's been through, can you?'

'No.' She bit her lip. 'So what should I do? Should I go and see him and try to find out if what you say is right, or what?'

'Only you can decide that, Heather. Nobody else can.' They had reached the end of the path and he stopped. 'The best advice I can give you is to follow your heart.'

'That's what Archie told me to do, too,' she whispered, her eyes filling with tears.

Ross bent and kissed her lightly on the cheek. 'Then what are you waiting for?'

He gave her a last smile then headed up to the road but Heather didn't follow him. She sank down on the soft damp grass and thought about what he had said. Was she brave enough to go after Archie and ask him outright if he loved her? The thought of receiving a negative answer scared her, but could it be any worse than this desolation she felt at losing him? At least she would know, once and for all, if there was no hope. That had to be better than spending the rest of her life wondering.

She stood up, filled with a new resolve as she headed back to the house. She would do what both Archie and Ross had told her to do—follow her heart—and hope it would lead her to the one place she wanted to be. By Archie's side. For ever!

CHAPTER FOURTEEN

So THIS was it, then. In a few minutes' time he would be on his way.

Archie took a last look around the flat. Now that the time had come, he felt relieved to be going. For nearly two years his life had been in a state of limbo, but not any more. It was as though all the heartache and guilt he'd suffered had been packed away into the back of the removal van and he was free to get on with his life. If it weren't for the fact that he desperately missed Heather, he would have looked forward to what the future held in store for him.

He sighed as he shut the front door. He hadn't heard a word from Heather since the previous weekend. He had hoped that she would turn up for his leaving party but there'd been no sign of her. He had phoned the agency that morning, but all he'd got had been the standard reply about it not being company policy to give out information about their staff. He had no idea what had happened to her and he couldn't help worrying.

He stopped at the porters' desk and arranged to have any mail forwarded to him then left the building. He had a long drive ahead of him and he had been intending to get an early start but all of a sudden he knew that he couldn't leave without seeing Heather first. The traffic was fairly light for once and it didn't take him long to reach her flat. He parked outside then ran down the steps and knocked on the door, mentally rehearsing what he would say. Something low-key would be best. He definitely wouldn't mention what had gone on last Saturday…

His mind made a lightening-fast swoop back to that moment when Heather had told him that she loved him and his heart contracted with sudden fear. What if she'd been telling him the truth? What if she *hadn't* been confused about her feelings? The thought that he might have rejected her love was too painful to bear and he rapped on the door again. Forget low-key, he was going to sort this out!

'She's not in.'

Archie swung round when a voice hailed him from the pavement and found an elderly woman watching him. From the number of carrier bags she was clutching, he assumed she was on her way back from the shops.

'What time did she go out?' he asked, hurrying up the steps.

'It must have been around four p.m. I heard a horn and looked out of the window to see what was happening,' she explained. 'There was a taxi parked outside and I saw the young lady get in.'

'You mean that she left last night?' Archie exclaimed in dismay.

'That's right. Around four in the afternoon,' she repeated helpfully. 'She had a bag with her so I assumed she was going away for the weekend.'

'I see. Thank you.'

Archie went back to his car. Had Heather gone home to Dalverston for the weekend? he wondered as he got in. But why had she decided to go home now? Was it because she'd wanted to see Ross?

His heart sank like a stone. It was the only explanation that made any sense. Heather had made it clear that she intended to get her life together before she went back home and he could only assume that she had done that now.

Had it been his rejection that had made her see how she really felt? The thought that she might have realised she was still in love with her ex-fiancé caused a physical ache in his guts but there was nothing he could do about it. After all, he was the one who had told her that she was mistaken about her feelings for him.

He started the engine, feeling the weight of his loss bearing down on him. Hard though it was, he had to accept that he had lost Heather for good.

It was late afternoon by the time Heather arrived back in London. There was a reduced service at the weekend and she'd had to wait hours for a train. She went straight to the taxi rank and told the driver to take her to Archie's flat, even though she had no idea what she was going to say to him. She'd tried opening her heart to him and it hadn't achieved very much, but there had to be a way to convince him that she was sincere. She loved him with all her heart and somehow she had to make him believe that!

It was the same porter on duty whom she'd met the first time Archie had taken her to his home. Although he let her in, Heather could tell that he was surprised to see her. She didn't let it deter her, however.

'Is Mr Carew in, Pete? I need to speak to him urgently.'

'I'm sorry, miss, but you're too late. He's already left.'

'Oh, I see. Do you know what time he'll be back? Maybe I can wait until he arrives.'

'I meant that he'd left for good. He went back home to Scotland this morning,' Pete informed her, looking a little embarrassed at having to break the news to her.

'I didn't realise he was leaving today!' she exclaimed. Panic engulfed her and she had to calm herself down before she could continue. 'Do you have a forwarding address for him? It's really important that I get in touch with him.'

'I'm sorry, miss. I wish I could help, but I'm not at liberty to hand out information like that. It's more than my job's worth.'

'I understand. I'm sorry. I didn't mean to put you on the spot,' Heather apologised.

She said goodbye and left, wondering what

she was going to do now. If Archie had wanted her to contact him, surely he would have made sure that she had his address? The fact that he hadn't bothered to give it to her proved that he had no interest in her. Pain washed through her as she walked along the street. She had followed her heart but it hadn't helped this time. It never could when Archie didn't love her.

Archie got halfway up the motorway before he realised that he couldn't leave things the way they were. He needed to see Heather and hear her tell him that she didn't love him or he would be for ever wondering if he'd made a terrible mistake.

He exited the motorway at the next junction and rejoined the southbound carriageway then drove all the way back. It was gone seven by the time he reached London and the first thing he had to do was find himself somewhere to stay as he couldn't go back to the flat. Apart from the fact that there was no furniture there, he'd arranged for the cleaning team to go in and get everything ready for the new tenant. He doubted if Heather would return until Sunday evening at the earliest, but it didn't matter. At some point she would have to come back and he intended to be there when she did.

He booked himself into a hotel and went straight up to his room and took a shower. Half an hour later he was on his way out again. He knew it was probably a waste of time going to Heather's flat but if there was a slim chance she hadn't gone away for the entire weekend, he didn't intend to let it pass him by. At the very least he could drop a note through her door telling her which hotel he was staying in. He took a cab rather than drive himself there and sat in the back, mentally rehearsing what he would say to her if she was there. He needed to convince her that he loved her and that she should give him a chance to prove it to her.

The streetlights were on when the cab

dropped him off. Archie paid the driver then ran down the basement steps and knocked on the door. It was only then that he realised there was a light on in the sitting room. When the door opened and Heather appeared, he felt the ground lift beneath his feet. All of a sudden every single word he had rehearsed on the way there disappeared from his head. He could only stand and stare at her in disbelief.

Heather felt the world suddenly tilt on its axis when she saw Archie standing outside the door. He was the last person she'd expected to see and the shock turned her mute. They stared at one another for several seconds before Archie cleared his throat.

'I called before and one of your neighbours told me that you'd gone away.'

'I went home,' she said, her voice sounding strained as it emerged from her lips.

'I thought that was where you must have gone.

To be honest, I didn't expect you would be back so soon. I just called round on the off-chance.'

'There were a couple of things I needed to do here,' she said, biting her lip when she realised what a massive understatement that was.

'And do those things have anything to do with me?'

He took a step towards her and her breath caught when she saw the way he was looking at her with such longing. When he reached out and touched her cheek, she closed her eyes, terrified that he would see the longing in her eyes, too. Archie had rejected her love once and she didn't think she could bear it if he rejected it a second time.

'I love you, Heather. I know I made a complete mess of things last weekend but please believe me. I love you so much and all I want is for you to be happy.'

'You love me?' Her eyes flew open and she stared at him in shock.

'Yes.' He smiled at her. 'I think I fell in love with you the first time I saw you sitting on that bench. I was just too confused about everything that had happened to appreciate how I felt. I know I hurt you by what I said last weekend, but I was afraid that you were rushing into a situation you would regret.'

'It worried me, too,' she admitted. 'I tried not to let it happen, Archie, but I had no control over my feelings. I fell in love with you and there isn't a thing I can do about it now. I shall love you for the rest of my life, with or without your consent.'

He gave a throaty chuckle as he swept her into his arms. 'Oh, there's no danger of me not consenting!'

He kissed her hungrily, showing her in the most effective way possible that he was telling her the truth. Heather clung to him as happiness welled up inside her and washed away the fear that had filled her this past week. Archie loved her and now there was nothing to stop them being together for good.

He raised his head and smiled into her eyes. 'Are you going to invite me in? I don't think your neighbour will be too happy if she sees what I have planned for the rest of the evening.'

Heather chuckled as she let him into the tiny hall. 'We certainly don't want to shock the neighbours.' She led him into the sitting room and closed the blind. 'There. Nobody can see what's going on now.'

'Good. This is strictly between you and me, and nobody else.'

He took her in his arms again, kissing her with a passion that soon had her clinging to him. They made love right there in the sitting room and it was a healing process for both of them. Heather knew that no matter what happened from this point on, they would get through it. They had their love to sustain them and that was all they needed.

Afterwards Archie went into her bedroom and

fetched the quilt, tucking it around them as they sat together on the sofa. 'I need to explain why I reacted the way I did last week when you told me that you loved me.'

Heather kissed his jaw, loving the feel of his body pressed against hers. She felt so safe when she was with him, as though nothing could hurt her ever again. 'I understand why you said what you did. You were afraid that I was rushing into something I would regret.'

'Yes. I couldn't bear to think that you would feel guilty when you realised you'd made a mistake. I also couldn't face the thought of going through what I'd been through before,' he added truthfully.

'With Stephanie?'

'It was a huge shock when I discovered that she and Duncan had fallen in love with each other. I had no inkling that she was unhappy let alone anything else.' He sighed. 'The truth is that I was too bound up in my work to notice what was going on. Work came first with me and everything else came a poor second, including Stephanie. No wonder she got fed up and sought happiness with someone else.'

'These things happen, Archie,' she said softly.

'I know they do.' He kissed her on the lips. 'But I think it proves that my feelings for Stephanie weren't as strong as they should have been. I will never put you second, Heather. You will always be my first priority because I love you so much. I never felt this way about Stephanie and I think she knew it, too. Even if she and Duncan hadn't fallen in love, our relationship wouldn't have lasted.'

'I don't know what to say.' She kissed him again, held him close for a moment, then sat back. 'I feel the same way about Ross. I saw him this morning and I realised that I had never actually been in love with him. I love him as a friend but that's all. What I feel for him is nothing compared to how I feel about you, Archie.'

'So you're sure you did the right thing by not marrying him?'

'Completely sure.'

'Good.' He kissed her on the mouth, showing her just how much that meant to him. Heather was trembling when he drew back and he smiled at her, his eyes filled with love. 'I love you so much, Heather Thompson. You've turned my life around in the past few weeks. After we talked about the accident, I felt so much better, as though I could move on with my life. Guilt was eating me up before but now I can see that I wasn't solely to blame for what happened.'

'I'm glad,' she said simply. 'You deserve to be happy, Archie. You deserve to make the choices you want, and not base them on a need to make amends.'

'And that's exactly what I'm going to do from now on.' He kissed the tip of her nose then smiled at her. 'You're such a wise woman for your tender years.'

'Wise?' She snorted with laughter. 'I don't think so!'

'Well, I do. Wise and beautiful.'

Another lingering kiss followed. Heather was drifting blissfully away on a sea of happiness when he raised his head again.

'I intend to reassess what I want from life in the future,' he told her huskily, obviously as affected as she was. 'I'll make sure the estate is being run properly, but I no longer feel that I have to sacrifice my career to achieve that. Hopefully, in a few months' time I shall be able to go back to what I enjoy most of all.'

'It would be such a shame if you gave up medicine, Archie. You have so much to offer the children in your care. They need you.'

'Thank you. I only hope you feel the same way and need me, too.' He looked deep into her eyes. 'I don't want us to be apart, Heather, so do you think you could move to Scotland with me? I know it's a lot to ask. Giving up your life here will be a wrench and—'

She stopped him the most expedient way she

knew—with a kiss. 'I don't care where I live so long as we're together.'

'You really mean that?' He gave a whoop of delight when she nodded. Gathering her into his arms, he held her close. 'How soon can you get packed?'

'As soon as you like. I can start now if that's what you want.'

Archie shook his head. 'I think we can wait a couple more hours.'

'Is that right? Why? Have you something better planned for the rest of the evening?'

'I most certainly have.' He stood up and lifted her in his arms then headed for the bedroom. 'I have plans for the rest of the evening and the night!'

EPILOGUE

Scotland: August

HEATHER stood by the window, looking out at the view over the loch. Evening was drawing in and the mountains had taken on a purplish haze. In another half an hour it would be completely dark.

Excitement unfurled inside her as she thought about what was going to happen then. She and Archie were getting married that night in the tiny chapel in the grounds of the estate. It was a tradition that all Carew weddings took place after the sun had set, Archie had explained to her, and she'd been more than happy to agree their wedding should take place then, too.

Everything was ready and now she was waiting for the time when she would become his wife.

A smile curved her mouth as she thought about how wonderful the past few months had been. Moving to Scotland had given them time to cement their relationship and every day they had been together they had grown closer. Archie was the man she would love until her dying day and she was just so relieved that she had realised it. When the drawing-room door opened and he came in, she smiled at him with a wealth of love in her eyes.

'It's nearly time, isn't it?'

'Just another few minutes and then we can set off to the chapel.' He took her in his arms and kissed her. 'Has anyone told you how gorgeous you look?' he murmured.

'Nobody who matters,' she replied, smiling up at him.

She'd been delighted with her dress but it was good to know that Archie liked it, too. Made from pure white silk, it was simply cut with a fitted bodice and a long flowing skirt that swept the ground. Over her shoulder, she had pinned a length of tartan plaid in the Carew family colours. The gardener's wife had made her a hand-tied bouquet of white roses and heather, and she had more heather woven into her hair. She felt like a fairy-tale princess about to be claimed by her prince, especially when Archie looked so dashing in his kilt.

'You look gorgeous.' He kissed her again, then put his arm around her as they looked out of the window. 'It's beautiful here, isn't it? I'm going to miss it when we move to Edinburgh.'

'I will, too, but we'll be able to pop back for weekends.' She turned to him. 'You're not sorry that you agreed to take this new job, are you, Archie?'

'Definitely not. The past few months have been wonderful. I've enjoyed being here and getting everything running properly again. It's something I needed to do, but now that I've found a manager capable of taking over, it leaves me free to pick up my career again.' He hugged her to his side and she could hear the excitement in his voice as he continued. 'Being given the chance to set up this new paediatric unit is more than I could have dreamed of, and I have you to thank for it, Heather. I would never have reached this point without you.'

'We're good for each other, Archie,' she said simply.

'We are. Very good indeed.' He kissed her again then held out his hand. 'It's time we set off for the chapel. We don't want to keep everyone waiting, do we?'

'Definitely not.'

Heather slipped her hand into his and let him lead her out of the house. Torches had been lit along the route they had to take, lighting their path. Most of the estate workers were there to watch them getting married, and they clapped as she and Archie walked past. When they reached the tiny chapel, she discovered that it was lit by hundreds of candles. The flickering glow from their flames cast a magical beauty over the place.

She turned to Archie and smiled. 'Thank you so much for doing all this for me. It's just like a fairy tale.'

'It's what you deserve, my darling.'

He kissed her softly on the lips then handed her over to her father, who was waiting by the door to escort her up the aisle. Heather's heart swelled with happiness as she walked towards her future husband. She felt so lucky and so blessed to have found Archie. She would never take their love for granted but cherish it every single day.

When Archie turned and held out his hand, she didn't hesitate. There were no second thoughts this time, no doubts, just a lifetime of happiness to look forward to. She placed her hand in his and knew that from this moment on they would be together for ever.

MEDICAL™

—∿— *Large Print* —∿—

Titles for the next six months…

January

VIRGIN MIDWIFE, PLAYBOY DOCTOR — Margaret McDonagh

THE REBEL DOCTOR'S BRIDE — Sarah Morgan

THE SURGEON'S SECRET BABY WISH — Laura Iding

PROPOSING TO THE CHILDREN'S DOCTOR — Joanna Neil

EMERGENCY: WIFE NEEDED — Emily Forbes

ITALIAN DOCTOR, FULL-TIME FATHER — Dianne Drake

February

THEIR MIRACLE BABY — Caroline Anderson

THE CHILDREN'S DOCTOR AND THE SINGLE MUM — Lilian Darcy

THE SPANISH DOCTOR'S LOVE-CHILD — Kate Hardy

PREGNANT NURSE, NEW-FOUND FAMILY — Lynne Marshall

HER VERY SPECIAL BOSS — Anne Fraser

THE GP'S MARRIAGE WISH — Judy Campbell

March

SHEIKH SURGEON CLAIMS HIS BRIDE — Josie Metcalfe

A PROPOSAL WORTH WAITING FOR — Lilian Darcy

A DOCTOR, A NURSE: A LITTLE MIRACLE — Carol Marinelli

TOP-NOTCH SURGEON, PREGNANT NURSE — Amy Andrews

A MOTHER FOR HIS SON — Gill Sanderson

THE PLAYBOY DOCTOR'S MARRIAGE PROPOSAL — Fiona Lowe

MILLS & BOON®
Pure reading pleasure™

x

1208 LP 2P P1 Medical

MEDICAL™

Large Print

April

A BABY FOR EVE	Maggie Kingsley
MARRYING THE MILLIONAIRE DOCTOR	Alison Roberts
HIS VERY SPECIAL BRIDE	Joanna Neil
CITY SURGEON, OUTBACK BRIDE	Lucy Clark
A BOSS BEYOND COMPARE	Dianne Drake
THE EMERGENCY DOCTOR'S CHOSEN WIFE	Molly Evans

May

DR DEVEREUX'S PROPOSAL	Margaret McDonagh
CHILDREN'S DOCTOR, MEANT-TO-BE WIFE	Meredith Webber
ITALIAN DOCTOR, SLEIGH-BELL BRIDE	Sarah Morgan
CHRISTMAS AT WILLOWMERE	Abigail Gordon
DR ROMANO'S CHRISTMAS BABY	Amy Andrews
THE DESERT SURGEON'S SECRET SON	Olivia Gates

June

A MUMMY FOR CHRISTMAS	Caroline Anderson
A BRIDE AND CHILD WORTH WAITING FOR	Marion Lennox
ONE MAGICAL CHRISTMAS	Carol Marinelli
THE GP'S MEANT-TO-BE BRIDE	Jennifer Taylor
THE ITALIAN SURGEON'S CHRISTMAS MIRACLE	Alison Roberts
CHILDREN'S DOCTOR, CHRISTMAS BRIDE	Lucy Clark

 MILLS & BOON®
Pure reading pleasure™

1208 LP 2P P2 Medical